"Are you asking me on a date? Is that allowed? I mean, you're a pastor. Can you date?"

Scott looked stunned by Trista's question, before he chuckled. "Yes. I have a special dispensation."

A date? With him? Not a good idea. "I'm not looking for a relationship."

He looked relieved. "Neither am I. Then how about if we meet at the theater? Just two friends watching the same movie. Not a date."

"That would work."

As Trista left the coffee shop, she couldn't believe she'd agreed to meet a pastor at the movies. Her family was going to laugh until they cried.

* * *

A Tiny Blessings Tale: Loving families and needy children continue to come together to fulfill God's greatest plans!

Books by Terri Reed

Love Inspired

Loves Comes Home #258
A Sheltering Love #302
A Sheltering Heart #362
A Time of Hope #370
Giving Thanks for Baby #420

Love Inspired Suspense

Strictly Confidential #21
*Double Deception #41
Beloved Enemy #44

*The McClains

TERRI REED

At an early age Terri Reed discovered the wonderful world of fiction and declared she would one day write a book. Now she is fulfilling that dream and enjoys writing for Steeple Hill Books. Her second book, *A Sheltering Love,* was a 2006 RITA® Award finalist and a 2005 National Reader's Choice Award finalist. She is an active member of both Romance Writers of America and American Christian Fiction Writers. She resides in the Pacific Northwest with her college-sweetheart husband, two wonderful children and an array of critters. When not writing, she enjoys spending time with her family and friends, gardening and playing with her dogs.

You can write to Terri at P.O. Box 19555, Portland, OR 97280 or visit her on the Web at www.terrireed.com or www.loveinspiredauthors.com.

Giving Thanks for Baby
Terri Reed

Steeple Hill®

Published by Steeple Hill Books™

Special thanks and acknowledgment are given
to Terri Reed for her contribution to the
A TINY BLESSINGS TALE miniseries.

STEEPLE HILL BOOKS

Steeple
Hill®

ISBN-13: 978-0-373-87456-9
ISBN-10:   0-373-87456-1

GIVING THANKS FOR BABY

www.SteepleHill.com

Printed in U.S.A.

Give thanks to the Lord, for He is good;
For His loving kindness is everlasting.
—*Psalms* 136:1

I want to thank my fellow writers in this series, Deb, Dana, Linda, Kathryn and Jillian for their input and support. It was fun working with you ladies.

Leah, Lissa and Melissa, I couldn't have made this book happen without your support and encouragement. Thanks bunches!

Chapter One

"If I had that window in my office, I wouldn't get any work done."

Trista Van Zandt glanced up from her homemade turkey and cheddar sandwich to smile at her tall blond sister-in-law who'd entered her office.

Kelly Van Zandt, beautiful in a rust-colored maternity dress that made the November leaves outside look drab in comparison, sat in one of the straight-backed chairs facing Trista's desk.

"It is lovely," Trista agreed. "Much better than the view of the parking lot I had in Richmond."

As a litigator for the law firm of Benson and Benson Trista's office on the fourth floor was small but had a nice view of the James River.

"One more good thing about you and Aidan moving here." Kelly smiled. "How is my nephew?"

Tenderness welled up in Trista's chest at the thought of her seven-month-old son, Aidan, who at the moment was safely at Chestnut Grove Child Care Center. "Adjusting well to day care. But anxious to see his new cousin."

Kelly rubbed her burgeoning belly. "Just a month to go."

Trista was glad that her brother's wife would have a calm and peaceful last month before giving birth, so unlike the final month of her own pregnancy. "Is everything okay?" she asked.

Kelly brushed back her thick blond hair and smiled. "Yes. I was out shopping for the baby the other day. I bought the cutest coming-home outfit in a neutral cream with bunnies, since I don't know if I'm bring home little Carissa or little Cameron. I'm so tempted to find out now what we're having."

"Don't. Believe me, the wait is worth it."

"So, how are *you* doing?" Kelly asked.

Trista had been expecting the question. Ever since she'd arrived in town, her brother, Ross and his wife, Kelly, had made it their job to take care of her and Aidan. As if they had the time, what with running Tiny Blessings adoption agency, Ross's private investigation firm and their own baby's imminent arrival. Trista shrugged. "Same old, same old."

"That's what I was afraid of," Kelly grumbled.

"Excuse me?"

Concern darkened Kelly's brown eyes. "I'm worried about you. You've done nothing but work and take care of Aidan. Why don't you let us babysit him this weekend while you go have some harmless fun?"

Trista mentally scoffed. Harmless fun wasn't something she had much experience with. Growing up in Brooklyn with alcoholic parents, she'd spent too much time running wild and getting in trouble. She always relied on her big brother to bail her out.

Once she'd realized the only way to find the security she'd lacked growing up was through her own determination and work, she'd applied herself to her studies.

She had an aptitude for litigation, and becoming a lawyer had seemed the best way to provide a stable life for herself. She'd be in control of her circumstances and have a decent salary. What more could she ask for?

But then she'd met Kevin Hughes at the end of her second year of law school and that blew having a stable life to pieces. She'd fallen hard for his charm and charisma and married him against Ross's advice.

Well, she'd learned her lesson.

Love and happily-ever-after, she decided, were unrealistic aspirations for her. Only a very few, like Ross and Kelly, ever obtained true happiness.

Now her life's goal was to provide a stable and secure home for her son. No matter what.

"You and Ross are the ones who should be going out now while you have the time," she stated. "Once the baby arrives, you'll understand why I choose to stay home at night with Aidan rather than doing anything else."

Kelly nodded in understanding. "Okay, then. How about joining Naomi's project?"

"Who is Naomi and what is her project?"

Sitting forward with an eager expression, Kelly explained. "Reverend Fraser's wife, Naomi, created a Christian friends Web site called The Kingdom Room for singles so people all over the state can connect via the Internet. That would be a perfect way for you to get to know someone without having to go on dates."

Shaking her head, Trista stated, "I'm not looking for a relationship. Been there, done that and not doing it again."

"Oh, honey, don't let what happened with Kevin sour you on love. I know God has someone in mind for you."

Trista refrained from commenting on the ludicrous notion that God cared about her at all. If God thought anything about her it was that she wasn't worth His time.

Putting away the remnants of her lunch, Trista came around the square glass-topped desk. "Don't worry about me. I have Aidan and you and Ross. That's all I need."

Kelly sighed as she pushed up from the chair. "At least say you'll come to dinner on Saturday."

"Of course." Trista gave Kelly a quick hug. "But I'll cook for you."

Kelly grinned. "Your lasagna?"

Trista grinned back, liking the sense of being valued coursing through her. "If that's what you want."

Kelly nodded eagerly. At the door, she paused. "Just think about The Kingdom Room. You might actually enjoy it."

"I'll think about it," Trista said to appease her sister-in-law.

As soon as Kelly left, Trista returned to her desk and opened a file folder on a pending civil case, but her thoughts returned to Kelly's words. *God has someone in mind for you.*

She ran a hand through her dark hair, which she'd worn loose today, and tried to concentrate on the papers in front of her. She hated to admit it, but deep down inside she wished what Kelly had stated about God was true.

But it wasn't. Not for her.

She'd only leave herself open to hurt if she let such thoughts crowd her brain. Her gaze shifted away from the unread file and came to rest on her computer.

An online singles group? An interesting idea.

But please! Some lonely hearts club was the last thing she needed in her life.

The first week of November was a busy time for assistant pastor Scott Crosby. Organizing a toy drive with the youth of Chestnut Grove Community Church took a great deal of patience and perseverance. Two things Scott struggled with.

Not that he minded pinch hitting for the Youth Minister, Caleb Williams. After all, serving the Lord was Scott's priority in life. And Scott didn't begrudge Caleb taking his family on vacation until after Thanksgiving.

The Youth Center buzzed with activity. Normally, the center resembled the inside of a YMCA, complete with an exercise room, a television room sporting comfy secondhand couches and beanbag chairs, an arts-and-crafts room with tons of supplies for the many art projects offered and a small cafeteria.

Today, however, the center looked more like Santa's workshop. The place was bursting with toys, wrapping paper, kids and…what *was* Naomi's little dog doing?

Scott made a grab for the long-bodied, short-legged animal as it ran past him with a curly-haired doll hanging from its jaws. "Whoa, Buddy." He scooped up the dachshund. "That's not for you."

Fourteen-year-old Tiffany skidded to a halt beside him. Her freckled nose wrinkled up in exasperation. "He's such a rascal," she exclaimed and took the squirming dog from Scott.

As she held the animal in her plump arms, Scott pried the doll out of Buddy's mouth. Inspecting the doll, he shrugged. "Doesn't look too bad. His teeth didn't puncture the plastic."

"Hey, Pastor Scott, should we put together the tricycle?" Jeremy, the star athlete of the local high school, called from across the room.

Leaving Buddy to Tiffany's care, Scott waded through the mounds of toys and kids to where Jeremy and Billy stood beside an unopened box with the picture of a child's red trike on the front. Both boys wore what seemed to be the fad of the day, long basketball shorts and hooded sweat-shirts.

"Hmm. Good question. Let me ask Naomi if she has a specific child in mind for this and get back to you. In the meantime, I think the tire store downtown still has a box for us to pick up. Take some bags with you so you can leave the box there. That way people can continue to donate."

Jeremy nodded and nudged Billy. "We'll take my truck."

Scott watched the boys leave. Pride filled his chest for the way the senior boy, Jeremy, was providing such a good role model for the younger, troubled Billy.

He glanced around and spotted the Reverend's wife. Skirting the mayhem in the middle of the TV room, Scott headed toward where she sat on the floor putting the finishing touches on a wrapped gift. Naomi's short-cropped red hair sported a paisley bandana that tied at the top, the ends of which poked straight up like dog ears. A few gray strands of hair reflected the overhead light.

Scott smiled with affection at the woman he considered to be a second mother rather than his superior's wife. "How are we doing over here?"

His gaze took in the stacks of pretty wrapped

gifts surrounding Naomi and the two young girls sitting in a semicircle on the floor.

Naomi looked up, her vivid blue eyes twinkling. "Did you ever imagine we'd have this many gifts after only three days?"

Scott chuckled. "No. The generosity of this town is a blessing."

They'd only distributed the donation boxes to the many willing businesses around the community of Chestnut Grove the previous Friday night. Now on Monday afternoon, the outpouring of donations surprised them all.

This was a community of friends and family who pulled together to take care of each other. Scott felt blessed to be serving the Lord in Chestnut Grove. Here, at least, he was accepted, flaws and all.

"At this rate we'll be able to put a toy in every underprivileged child's hand at Christmas for miles around," Naomi stated and held out her hand to Scott.

He helped her to her feet. She shook out her legs. "Whew, sitting on the floor at my age isn't a good idea."

One of the teenage girls giggled.

"You're not old," another girl, Nikki, commented. "At least you don't act old. Not the way my parents do."

The compliment was as close as the girl had come to saying she cared. Scott knew Naomi had been doing her level best to break through the teen's protective barriers. Nikki liked to dress in all black and considered herself an Emo. When Scott was younger the term had been Goth. But whatever the phrase of the day it still conveyed the emotional chaos and confusion he remembered.

Naomi touched Nikki's blond head in affection. "You girls carry on while Scott and I have a chat."

She led Scott to the vacant cafeteria where she poured herself a cup of coffee. Scott declined her offer and took a seat at the round eating table. "The kids were wondering what to do with the boxed tricycle."

Naomi sipped her coffee. "Leave it for now."

"Okay." He trusted Naomi's judgment. Reverend Fraser was blessed to have such a good wife. Scott hoped one day he'd find a soul mate, someone willing to serve the Lord along side of him. Someone who'd accept him as he was, without trying to change him the way Sylvia had. She'd been his one serious girlfriend from high school through college until he'd decided to go into the ministry.

She'd dumped him then, saying she wasn't

ready for a serious relationship. But Scott knew the truth. Sylvia hadn't wanted to be a pastor's wife.

Scott leaned forward to place his elbows on the table and press his palms together. "I just sent Jeremy and Billy to collect the toys from Paul's Tire Emporium. I figure next Saturday should be soon enough to have the kids out collecting from the bins around town again. I can't imagine we'll get much more than we already have."

Naomi gestured to him with her cup. "It was a brilliant idea on your part to start the drive early this year. We can get this done and out of the way so we can all enjoy the upcoming holidays ourselves."

Sometimes his impatience paid off. "I'm firming up plans with the food bank for the Thanksgiving dinner the church will be hosting. We need more volunteers, so if you could get the word out that would be great."

"I certainly will." She set her cup down and leaned forward. "How's your family?"

"Good. I talked to Mom yesterday. She made a point of telling me she expected me at the dinner table on Thanksgiving."

Scott would rather spend the majority of Thanksgiving Day helping feed those less fortunate than himself. At least that was the best explanation he could give his family. But the main reason he had declined to spend dawn till dusk at his parents' house was the constant teasing he took from his siblings.

Sometimes he could escape to the game room in the basement with all of his nieces and nephews, but even there he wasn't safe. His sibs would hunt him down.

Growing up the youngest of four, he'd always borne the brunt of the jokes and pranks. He didn't understand or appreciate the rough ribbing. He sometimes wondered if the taunting hid the fact that his brothers and sister hadn't wanted another sibling. He'd been a surprise for his parents, a fact his siblings loved to remind him.

It didn't help the family dynamics any that Scott wasn't cut from the same cloth as the rest of the high-achieving Crosbys. His father had been disappointed that Scott hadn't followed his siblings into a professional career. His mother clucked over him as if he was still in kindergarten.

All in all, spending time with his family was stressful for him.

Naomi's gaze turned speculative. "Scott, when are you going to find a nice girl and settle down?"

Scott coughed at the unexpected question. "I beg your pardon?"

"I worry that you work too hard. A young man should have some fun in his life. And you won't be young forever."

He didn't need the reminder, but hearing it stated out loud accentuated the mortality of life. His parents would be celebrating their fiftieth wedding anniversary soon. A rarity in this day and age. A feat Scott could only hope to replicate one day.

"Time flies, and if you aren't careful, you'll be wishing you'd spent a bit more time on yourself than on others," Naomi added.

Scott bristled. "I don't think serving the Lord is a waste of my time."

She gave him an indulgent look. "Don't put words in my mouth. Serving the Lord is wonderful, but a man of God like you needs a helpmate in life. God doesn't want all of us to be alone."

Uh-oh. Scott blinked. He knew the youth of the church had played matchmaker with the Youth Minister, Caleb, and Anne, the former church secretary, now Caleb's wife. It sounded as if Naomi wanted to pick up where they'd left off. Better put a stop to this pronto. He held up a hand. "I'm content with my life. Besides, I have so much on my plate with Caleb on vacation I think I should wait until the time is right."

"That excuse will only last so long you know," she commented with a gleam in her eyes.

Scott stood and backed away as if putting space between them might stop Naomi from whatever was going on in that head of hers. "I better get back to the kids."

He didn't want to give Naomi any chance to try to fix him up with someone in the congregation. That could jeopardize the acceptance he enjoyed in Chestnut Grove. Besides, he hadn't lied when he'd said he had too much on his plate right now. But he also hadn't wanted to admit he didn't know if the time to find a wife would ever be right. He would hate to disappoint another person that he loved.

Naomi watched Scott shoot out of the cafeteria as though the Hound of the Baskervilles was on his heels. The man certainly was gun-shy of relationships.

As far as she'd seen, Scott kept everyone at an emotional arm's length, even while he'd bend over backward to be of help. She understood how hard his decision to follow God's call into ministry was on his relationship with his family and knew there was a rift or something that needed healing. But she sensed loneliness and a deep hurt in Scott, as well.

"Lord, how would You have me help this young man?"

Naomi waited a beat. An idea formed in her mind. "Ah, yes. Thank You, Lord."

She knew what to do.

After washing her cup out and putting it on the drain pad, she went to her office where she fired up her computer. With a few clicks and some creative thinking, she added Scott anonymously to the growing number of members in The Kingdom Room.

"Sometimes people need a little help recognizing that the right time is right *now*," she stated aloud and sat back. Now all she had to do was wait and watch the fun happen.

"Go to sleep and good night, my sweet prince," Trista cooed softly to Aidan as she gently laid him in his crib. The teddy bear motif on the bumpers and mobile included little cubs frolicking in the grass and always made her smile. She'd found the crib and bedding at a secondhand store in Richmond. They were perfect for her little boy.

She tucked the blanket more securely around Aidan. Heartbreaking joy squeezed her chest, bringing tears to her eyes. She touched the downy softness of his dark hair. If anything were ever to happen to him, she didn't think she could take it.

"Oh, God, if You're real, please watch over this little life," she whispered with a small hiccuping sob.

Aidan stirred. She quickly backed away to keep from disturbing him further. He needed his sleep. She did, too, but sleep had become hard to find ever since Aidan's birth. She was terrified he'd need her in the middle of the night. She'd read all the baby books she could find and still feared that something bad would happen.

Being a parent was the most nerve-racking thing she'd ever experienced and she could only imagine that her anxiety would grow along with Aidan.

The sound of the phone ringing in the living room made her wince. Quickly, she left Aidan's room, keeping the door cracked open, and rushed to answer the phone.

"Hello?"

Silence greeted her.

Trista frowned. "Hello? Is someone there?"

Straining to listen, she swore she heard the sound of muffled sobs as if the person on the other end of the line were trying to keep their tears quiet. Then the line went dead.

An eerie chill crept up Trista's spine as she replaced the receiver. She didn't know who had her number other than Kelly, Ross and her office. Fearing something had happened to her brother or his wife, she quickly snatched up the receiver and dialed their home number.

"Hi," her brother's booming voice intoned.

"Is everything okay?" Trista asked, skipping the pleasantries of greeting. She noted the blinking light of the answering machine. She'd forgotten to check it again when she'd come home from work.

"Yes. Why?"

She could hear the wariness in his voice. She couldn't blame him with all the problems that had plagued the adoption agency of late. First the discovery of so many adoption records having been falsified over the years. Then Kelly received that threatening note at the Fourth of July celebration, and less than three weeks later the offices had been broken into and set on fire.

And just last month, Ross's SUV's front windshield had been shattered and another note left behind, demanding they stop investigating the phony records. "Is Kelly there? Is she okay?"

"She is. Trista, what's going on?"

"Nothing." She rolled her tense shoulders and shifted the receiver to the other side of her head.

Her sweatshirt bunched up as she moved. She tugged at it. "I just received the strangest call. When I answered, there was no response, but I'm sure I heard crying."

"Hmm. Do you think Mom could have called you?"

Trista scoffed. "No. She can't even remember my name. How would she know where to call me?"

"I have no idea. But Alzheimer's is a strange disease."

A disease that was hereditary. A knot formed in her stomach. "Yes, well…be that as it may, I don't think it was Mom."

"It was probably a wrong number. I wouldn't worry too much about it. Whoever it was will call back if it was important," Ross commented. "Kelly says you're coming over Saturday to cook dinner."

"Yep. Kelly requested lasagna. Will you make one of your killer salads?"

"Of course. Hey, I was thinking of driving out to visit Mom on Sunday after church. Will you come?"

Trista closed her eyes as guilt and resentment warred in her heart. Ross was so good at visiting their mother in the nursing home outside of Richmond. For Trista, the visits were torture.

Michelle Van Zandt barely recognized her only daughter.

The last time Trista had gone to the home, Michelle had become so upset because she'd thought Trista was there to steal her husband away.

Henry Van Zandt had died from liver failure years ago. That their mother still worried her husband was cheating on her only served to instill in Trista a loathing to ever go down the matrimonial road again.

After her disaster of a marriage to Kevin and watching her mother's decline, Trista vowed to concentrate on her son to make sure he didn't grow up making the same mistakes his family made. She'd even bought a book on how to prevent Alzheimer's, for herself and Aidan.

"Trista?"

"Uh, I don't know. We'll see." That was as much commitment as she could give at the moment.

Ross sighed. "We can talk about it more on Saturday."

Perfect. Now she was going to have to endure his lecture on how she should forgive their parents for the past and how their mother needed them now. She was well practiced in tuning out her brother's lectures. "I'll see you Saturday."

She hung up and pushed the play button on the answering machine.

"Hi, babe. I need to talk with you. Call me, okay?"

Her ex-husband's voice filled the room and she clenched her teeth. With a sharp jab of her finger she deleted the message.

What did he want now? He'd given up total custody of their son in the divorce, in exchange for the condo and all their possessions. She didn't have anything else for him to take.

Restless and edgy, she cleaned the updated kitchen, straightened up Aidan's plethora of toys strewn around the apartment and channel surfed on the twenty-inch TV that Ross had bought for her as a welcoming gift. When that didn't relax her, she pulled out her laptop and set it on the pine coffee table. She could at least work.

Once the computer was ready she stared at the screen. She didn't want to work. Instead, she surfed the Internet looking for fun things to do with Aidan around town.

A local farm had a pumpkin patch and hayride day coming up. That would be good.

Hmm. Story time at the new bookstore downtown. Aidan loved listening to stories.

She drummed her fingers on the table. Ugh! She needed a manicure.

Maybe Kelly was right. She'd been working too hard and not taking care of herself. She wished she had a friend in town but that was another thing her marriage to Kevin had ruined.

He'd so monopolized every moment, getting upset when she wanted to spend time with her friends, that she'd eventually let the friendships fade. She didn't even know how to get hold of any of her old college gang.

She needed to link up with others who were in the same boat.

Single and lonely.

She frowned. She wasn't lonely. She had Aidan. She just needed someone to talk to.

What was the name of that online group Kelly mentioned?

The Kingdom Room.

Heart pounding with anticipation, she went to the Web site. She hesitated a moment before bolstering her courage and registering. After filling in the blanks and choosing a screen name, she was in.

For an hour she lurked, reading the posts from the last few days. Men and women both conversed about various aspects of being single. A few mentioned their children. Nothing overly personal or uncomfortable here.

Okay, this was doable.

She wasn't looking for a romantic encounter, just friends to understand.

With a deep breath, she jumped into the current thread of conversation, hoping to find someone out there to connect with.

Yet, a little voice inside her head taunted her—only more hurt would be her reward.

Chapter Two

By Tuesday morning Scott's e-mail in-box was bursting.

He stared at the amount of posts. What was going on?

After booting up the computer when he first walked into his office, he'd gone in search of some tea. Setting his mug of Earl Grey on the marble coaster on his mahogany desk, he slipped into his fabric-covered chair.

Normally, he took a moment to let the soothing hues of blues and brown in the office soothe his mind before turning his thoughts to work. But the staggering number of e-mails held his attention.

He clicked into the in-box and began to scroll through the e-mails. They were all addressed to *Called2serve*. A dawning realization clenched his gut as he read the posts. Someone, Naomi he was sure, had registered him to The Kingdom Room and added him to their e-mail loop.

He didn't have time for this.

His father had called just as he was leaving the apartment he rented in a private residence east of Main Street. The phone call had been strange. His father had asked if Scott would say a few words at his parents' fiftieth wedding anniversary. Scott could hear the emotion in his father's voice and it left Scott feeling off-kilter.

Joseph Crosby had always been as solid as a hundred-year-old oak tree and just as unbendable.

His father was a family practitioner in Richmond. He'd had a long career and a great reputation. Everyone knew Doc Crosby. Candice Crosby was a star in her own right as a skilled surgeon. Scott and his sibs never lacked for medical care.

Scott's sister, Elise, followed their father into medicine and was now a pediatrician. Her husband was a contractor and had built their home as well as Scott's two brothers' homes.

John and Kyle Crosby had veered from medicine and both became lawyers. An honorable profession according to their father.

And then there was Scott. The quiet one. The underachiever. The assistant pastor.

Another e-mail popped up.

Scott shook his head to clear his thoughts. He really didn't have time for an Internet singles group. He needed to focus on organizing the upcoming Thanksgiving Day dinner for the homeless.

But curiosity got the better of him; he couldn't help quickly scanning the e-mails before deleting them. Some were interesting threads of conversation regarding the holidays and the difficulty of being single when so many people seemed to expect couples at gatherings.

One post in particular grabbed his attention.

Hi, I'm new here and am hoping to connect with others who might understand. I've been divorced for a short time, but the marriage was over long before the official decree, I just didn't know it. So I'm starting over in a new city and between work and my baby, I don't have time to make friends. I'd been married since my second year of college. It's strange to be alone, especially as the holidays approach. I do have some family, but they have their own lives. I don't want to be a burden. Any suggestions? Is the emptiness I feel just the lack of a spouse? Is it normal? Will it pass?

Momof1

Scott sat back. These answers couldn't be found online or anywhere else on this earth. Naomi may have added him to The Kingdom Room for her own reasons, but God obviously had reasons, as well.

Scott didn't believe in coincidences. The *Momof1* needed a guide to lead her to the truth. To the fulfillment she craved.

Only doing it via the Internet seemed so…cold and distant. So unlike God.

But in an age of electronic devices… God met people where they were. And Scott would serve any way God wanted him to.

Scott closed his eyes. *Lord, give me the words You would have me say.*

A moment later, he began to type.

It was late in the night on Wednesday when Trista remembered to check her e-mail. The past couple of days had been hectic. The senior Benson had been pleased with the work she'd done on a small claims case that had settled well and had informed her he wanted her on a new case that was a complicated land issue between the county and their client.

So she'd spent every spare moment she could studying the land laws of Virginia and specifically their county.

Now that Aidan had gone to bed, she propped her feet up on the coffee table, squirmed into a comfortable position on the secondhand sofa and fired up her laptop.

Whoa! These Kingdom Room people had a lot of free time. She couldn't believe the amount of e-mail in her in-box.

She started with the first response from her post and slowly made her way through the quagmire of words. Some made her laugh, others she didn't know what to make of.

One man sent her his picture and asked for a date. She quickly deleted that. It creeped her out that some one would ask for a date without knowing anything about the other person. For all the guy knew, she could be a serial killer.

Several women said she was nuts to be feeling anything but glad to be single. Those posts made Trista wonder what had happened in their marriages. She and Kevin hadn't been very happy together, at least not the last few years, but she still missed having someone to talk to at the end of the day. Someone to share the ups and the downs with.

There were suggestions of places she could go to meet people, mostly exotic locales. Yeah, right!

She had a baby to take care of, she couldn't go gallivanting all over the world.

Books were recommended on dealing with divorce and single parenthood. Links to support groups were offered. A few commiserated on the emptiness and loneliness of finding themselves single after so many years of marriage.

Several said they'd be praying for her. She rolled her eyes at the clichéd sentiment. If only life's problems were fixed so easily.

"What did you expect?" she asked herself aloud. This was a Christian Web site. These people believed in the power of prayer. It certainly couldn't hurt to have them praying for her.

Trista wrote back to a few ladies that she felt a connection with, giving a brief glimpse into her life, yet careful not to reveal anything too personal.

A person just never knew who she was actually "talking" to online. Hadn't she just seen a news show about online predators?

Then one e-mail snagged her interest.

Momof1

Has your family said that you're a burden to them? If not, don't assume that's how they feel. One way of finding connections would be to join a women's group in your area. As to your question about emptiness…people are not only physical and emotional beings with a need for food and companionship, but humans are spiritual beings with a need for God. How is your relationship with Him?

Called2serve

Trista stared at the screen. It wasn't an unreasonable question that *Called2serve* asked. Presumably everyone on this site would believe in God. And it wasn't that she didn't believe in Him. It was just…where had God been when she was growing up and needed Him?

That was a question she was afraid to ask because she might find out she was right. She wasn't worth God's time.

Scott had thought he'd scared off *Momof1* when a day had passed without a reply. But there was a message from her in his in-box on Thursday evening. He clicked on the post.

Called2serve

You ask how my relationship is with God. I'm trying to discover that amid all the turmoil of my divorce.

Momof1

Compassion filled Scott's chest. He couldn't imagine the pain of divorce. The death of a marriage. The shattered dreams.

The only experience he had with matters of the heart had been Sylvia. They had met during high school in the choir at church and shared a love of music and God. At least he'd thought they had until she'd walked away from him and the life he'd offered.

Her rejection had hurt, but had faded quickly after he'd entered seminary. Since then, he hadn't met anyone whom he wanted to let into his heart.

He offered *Momof1* what solace he could even though he felt very inadequate.

Thursday night.

Momof1
   I don't know the circumstance of your situation, but I do know God loves you. His comfort and peace are gifts He wants to give you.
   Called2serve

Friday Morning.

Called2serve
   How do I receive these gifts?
   Momof1

* * *

Friday night.

Momof1

There's nothing complicated about it, even though we'd like to think there is. Open your heart and mind to Him. Ask Him silently or aloud to show you His love, to come into your life. He so longs to. Then you wait and watch. He'll reveal Himself. Sometimes in small ways, sometimes in big, dramatic ways. But you'll know. And you'll feel the peace and comfort like a gentle blanket of protection.

Called2serve

Trista entered The Kingdom Room on Friday night to discover a chat room was now available. She'd decided to stop corresponding with *Called2serve* since the direction of their conversation was heading into waters she wasn't ready to navigate. Asking God into her life?

She was too afraid He'd say no.

It took a moment to acclimate to the format of the chat, but soon she was in on the discussion of the latest blockbuster movie. She hadn't seen it, but asked if it was worth the time and trouble to go since she wasn't into action films.

She was surprised to see *Called2serve* enter the room. But *Called2serve* didn't acknowledge her, instead wrote that he wanted to see the movie and planned to go on Sunday afternoon.

Several other people who hadn't seen it yet said they too would make a point of seeing the movie over the weekend at their local theaters and then the discussion could resume.

All she could commit to was a quick, I'll think about it.

That earned her a smiley face from *Called2serve*.

For some reason that silly little yellow icon on her computer screen made her laugh.

Saturday morning arrived with a fresh fall of snow. Outside, a soft blanket of white covered the town of Chestnut Grove and a crisp freshness in the air brought anticipation of a cold winter. Scott stomped his snow-covered boots on the dry pavement beneath the awning of The Reading Rainbow Palace, downtown's newest bookstore and café.

Inside the double doors, warmth seeped beneath the collar of his coat. He quickly shed the down parka, draping it on a peg bolted to the wall alongside a dozen others.

The place was hopping with mothers and

children vying for spots near the center rise where a woman in a green vintage dress sat waiting. In her hands, she held a book and a puppet.

Hanging on to his backpack, Scott made his way to the counter and ordered a cappuccino with double whipped cream. Soon he was settled at a table off to the side where he pulled out a fiction book and began to read, the voices of the crowd fading into white noise.

A jarring knock against the table interrupted his flow. He glanced up and met the gaze of a beautiful, brunette woman with the most intense, bright-blue eyes he'd ever seen. She smiled apologetically as she maneuvered a jogging stroller to the corner before unstrapping an infant from the seat. The baby, dressed snugly in a powder-blue jumpsuit, had the same dark hair and vivid blue eyes as his mother. His chubby legs pumped as she held him face out.

The woman stood and stared at the crowd, indecision written plainly across her oval face. Scott didn't blame her for hesitating before venturing into the sea of bodies taking up every available space on the carpeted floor. The only vacant chair sat across from Scott. He waved a hand to garner the woman's attention.

She flicked her gaze at him, clearly unsure if

she wanted to give him her attention. Scott indicated the chair. She bit her lip for a second before pulling the chair out and plopping down in it.

"Thanks," she whispered.

"You're welcome," he whispered back.

The woman turned her gaze toward the storyteller. Scott turned his attention back to his book, but now the words wouldn't hold his interest. His gaze kept straying to the woman sitting across from him. He hadn't seen her in church.

He liked the way her dark ponytail hung low at the nape of her neck in a sleek way. The high arch of her cheekbones and forehead gave her face sharp lines that were softened by her pert nose and dark lashed eyes. She wore a red turtleneck sweater and close-fitting black pants tucked into her snow boots.

There was an air of sophistication about her, yet she didn't come across like one of the many debutantes his mother had always tried to fix him up with.

She glanced his way and he quickly picked up his drink to mask his bad manners. He usually didn't stare. Or notice a woman's left hand. Hers was surprisingly ringless.

But for some reason this woman drew his attention.

Probably it was the way she so deftly handled

her son, like a pro. And there was no mistaking the love shining in her expression every time she cooed in her child's ear.

Before the last story ended, the baby had fallen asleep, his little body curled over her arm, his head listing to the side. Scott tapped on the table, drawing the woman's questioning gaze.

Nodding his head toward the child, he whispered, "He's asleep."

The woman's eyes widened as she adjusted the infant so she could verify Scott's statement. With a rueful shake of her head, she said softly, "So much for story time."

She made to rise and Scott quickly asked, "Can I buy you a coffee?"

Slowly, she sat back. For a moment she stared at him, then finally she nodded. "Decaf almond latte."

Scott rose and made his way to the counter. Naomi was going to love to hear that he'd just offered to buy this woman coffee without even asking her name. But the moment he'd thought she was leaving, he'd plunged ahead with the first thought that came to mind.

He ordered the drink and a few minutes later returned to the table. The jogging stroller was now pulled close to the table and the baby sleeping soundly in the seat.

Scott set the mug in front of the woman before he sat down. The quiet hum of parents helping their children do a craft that related to the story swirled around them.

She smiled as she put her slender hands around the mug. "Thank you. This was thoughtful."

"You're welcome." Keeping his voice low, even though the crowd was busy with parents and kids wanting the storyteller's books, he held out his hand. "Scott Crosby."

She slipped her hand into his, the temperature from the mug having heated her palm. Warmth spread up his arm.

"I'm Trista Van Zandt."

"Any relation to Ross and Kelly?"

Her expressive eyes widened. "Ross is my big brother. Do you know them?"

"Yes, very well. Are you visiting?"

She trailed a fingertip around the top of the mug.

"No, I moved here recently from Richmond."

To make sure he wasn't making an incorrect assumption, because some women didn't take their husband's names, he asked, "Are you and your husband enjoying our small community?"

Trista's expression closed. "I'm divorced."

"Oh. I'm sorry."

She gave him a tight smile. "Nothing for you to feel sorry about."

He acknowledged that with a nod. "Does your ex-husband still live in Richmond?"

"Yes, thankfully. He wasn't ready to be a father. The very idea cramped his style."

Anger stirred in Scott's soul. "That's just…" He was tempted to say a bad word but resisted with effort. "I'll never understand how some men can be so selfish. Being a parent is the greatest honor God gives us."

She blinked, obviously surprised by his words. "I suppose that's true. It certainly is the hardest job I've ever had."

"It's good you have your brother and Kelly so close by. Are *you* adjusting to life here, then?"

Her smile was warm. "Yes, thank you. The slower pace is perfect for Aidan and me. I love my job and Aidan seems to like his day care."

"Where are you working?"

"Benson and Benson."

"Ah, are you a lawyer?" Scott said, wondering why that wouldn't surprise him. She had a very strong self-possessed way about her, similar to

Scott's brothers. Only on them, it could, at times, come across as arrogance.

"Yes. And you? What do you do, Scott?" Her interested gaze sought answers.

Scott gladly gave one. "I'm the assistant pastor at Chestnut Grove Church."

She blinked. "Oh."

Scott could feel her retreat like the rays of the sun going behind a cloud. A disquieting sense of disappointment engulfed him, though why he didn't understand.

It shouldn't bother him that this woman would put up a wall between them because of his call to follow God. So many other people in his life had, as well.

He sighed. "I take it you don't go to church?"

She raised a brow. "Why would you say that?"

He shrugged. "The vibe you're giving off."

One side of her mouth rose. "Oh, really? I didn't know pastors bought into vibes."

"Reading people is part of the job."

"Then you must be good at your job, because you're right, I don't attend church. My parents weren't big on religion and I just never got into it, not like Ross has."

Scott considered her for a moment. "Now that

you've moved here, maybe you should consider attending. You might be surprised."

She lifted one slim shoulder. "Maybe." She fiddled with a napkin. "I read in the paper that the Douglas Matthews show will be filming at the upcoming food drive that the church is hosting. That must be exciting to have that kind of coverage."

"Yes, it is." She didn't fool Scott by changing the focus of their conversation. "The Douglas Matthews Show has brought Chestnut Grove a lot of attention. I think the food drive this year will be the biggest yet. And the Thanksgiving Day dinner for the homeless is sure to be a success." He eyed her speculatively. "We could use more volunteers if you're interested."

She seemed to consider his words. "I might be. I'll have to get back to you on that."

"Call the church and ask for Naomi. She'll be able to get you plugged in."

"I'll think about it." She took a sip of coffee.

An awkward moment of silence stretched between them.

"Did you grow up here?" she asked.

He shook his head. "I was born here, but we moved to Richmond when I was a teen. I came back as soon as I left seminary." He searched her face. "What about you? Where were you born?"

"Brooklyn, New York. I went to college at Columbia, then moved to Richmond, where my ex-husband's family is from."

Scott's gaze touched on the sleeping baby. "How old is…Aidan?"

Affection lit up her eyes. "Yes, Aidan. He's seven months."

"That's a fun age. They aren't supermobile yet, but their personalities start to develop."

Both of her eyebrows rose. "You sound like you know kids. Are you married?"

He laughed. "No. I just know from all my nieces and nephews."

"Ah. Learning secondhand. My big brother's been learning from Aidan. I can't wait to see Ross with his own little one."

"They'll be good parents," Scott stated. "Tiny Blessings has been through the wringer with all the scandals that have happened over the past few years. But your sister-in-law and brother seem to be handling it wonderfully."

Trista's chest puffed with pride. "They are. I've been trying to help a little with some of the legal stuff, but it gets very complicated and time-consuming. Not to mention how emotionally involving it is."

"I can imagine. The agency has been a blessing to so many people."

Trista liked the way he put that. In fact, she liked Scott. His blond, green-eyed good looks aside, there was something very soothing and gentle about him that was so unlike her brother or Kevin.

She supposed being a pastor was the difference.

And being a pastor also made him off-limits.

That is, if she were looking for a relationship, which she wasn't. She couldn't imagine two people having more dissimilar perspectives on life.

Beside her Aidan stirred. She picked him up and snuggled him close as he awakened.

"You're very good with him," Scott commented.

The compliment made her heart swell. "I can't imagine my life without him now."

She dug through the stroller bag and brought out a baby bottle with powdered formula in it. She turned to Scott. "Would you mind holding him while I fill the bottle with water?"

Scott's eyes lit up. "I'd love to, if you think he'll do okay with a stranger."

"Only one way to find out," she quipped and handed her son to him.

Scott handled the baby as if he'd been doing it forever. He bounced Aidan on his knee and made faces until Aidan giggled.

Trista went to the counter to get water, her gaze straying to Scott and Aidan. She trusted Scott with her son, which was unusual. Again, the fact that he was a pastor must be the reason she felt so comfortable with him.

She watched them together, Aidan's eyes bright with curiosity and Scott so animated. She felt a pang of sadness and anger for what Kevin had chosen to destroy.

He'd vowed to have nothing to do with their child if she chose to keep him. So far he'd kept his vow.

But the disturbing message left on her machine earlier in the week nagged at her. Thankfully, he hadn't called again and she had no intention of calling him. She was done with that chapter of her life. She and Aidan would do just fine.

She thanked the girl behind the counter who handed her some lukewarm water. She quickly mixed Aidan's bottle and went back to the table.

Scott reached for the bottle. "May I?"

"Uh, sure." She watched as Aidan greedily sucked from the rubber tip, drips of liquid leaking from the corners of his mouth. She handed Scott a burp cloth. He dabbed at the corners of Aidan's mouth and placed the cloth underneath the bottle to catch the dribbles.

"Your sister must love to have you babysit," Trista commented.

Scott chuckled. "I get asked to babysit a lot. Not only by my siblings' kids but at church, too." He shrugged. "I love kids."

"It shows." Her heart twisted with yearning for someone like Scott to be an important part of her son's life. Maybe he could be, as their friend? That might require attending church, but more significantly, letting Scott into her life. She wasn't sure if she could do either one.

Chapter Three

Trista's attention was snagged by a woman and a young boy as they rose from a nearby table. If she wasn't mistaken, it was Lynda Matthews—television talk show star Douglas Matthews's wife—and their son, Logan. Trista gasped softly as the woman turned toward her.

A dark bruise covered one eye from the bottom of her cheekbone to the top of her eyebrow, masking the spattering of freckles on the left side of her face.

Trista jumped up and went to the woman. "Lynda? What happened?"

Lynda's pale-blue eyes widened in panic. She reached up and tugged at her light-brown bobbed hair as if to cover the mark. Her four-year-old son clung to her hand.

"I—I, uh…" She tried to smile but it looked more like a wince. "Logan has a great pitching arm."

Trista didn't buy the lie. No way could Logan, a little slip of a boy, throw a baseball hard enough to cause such damage.

Scott joined them, Aidan propped on his hip as though he belonged there, but his jaw had taken on a hard edge. "Hello, Mrs. Matthews. Logan. Would you care to join us?"

Lynda shook her head and clutched at the closed neckline of her button-up blouse with her free hand. "We really should go. Douglas has an interview this morning with the paper and he would…like for us to be home when he gets home."

Trista had met Douglas Matthews on several occasions. She doubted the self-important man would even notice if his wife and son were home. At the Fourth of July barbecue in Winchester Park, Lynda had indicated she wanted to talk with Trista in a lawyer-client way.

But Lynda had never called.

Clearly something was going on, and Trista wasn't going to let it slide. "Lynda, would you be interested in having lunch with me one day next week?"

Lynda swallowed. Her gaze shifted around as if checking to see that no one overheard them. Timidly she nodded.

"Do you still have my card?" Trista asked, even as she stepped back to the stroller to find another one.

Lynda took the business card Trista held out with shaky hands. "We should go."

Trista stopped her with a hand to her arm. Lynda shied away slightly. "Promise me you'll call. That has all my numbers on it."

"I'll try," Lynda said softly.

"If I don't hear from you by Thursday, I'll call you."

Lynda shook her head. "Oh, no. I'll call." She scurried away, her son close to her side.

"Did you believe that story?"

Trista turned to Scott. Worry darkened his eyes. "What do your vibes tell you?"

A muscle ticked in his jaw. "That she's hiding something. Something not good."

Trista nodded. "That, Pastor Scott, is an understatement. I'd say her husband did that to her."

Scott frowned. "I wouldn't go advertising your suspicion unless you have proof."

She took offense to his warning to keep quiet. That wasn't in her nature. She took Aidan from him. "What other explanation could there be?"

Scott shook his head. "I don't know. I can only pray that it's not true and that she will get help if it is."

Hugging Aidan close to still the quiet anger running through her, Trista said, "She'll get help. I'll make sure of that."

Scott smiled. "Spoken like a true avenger." His expression turned cautious. "Just remember that revenge and vengeance aren't yours, hers or mine to take."

Trista refrained from rolling her eyes. "You sound like my brother. He uses scripture on me all the time and he's not even a pastor."

Scott's expression looked so stricken that she laughed.

"Don't worry, I know Ross is only trying to help me."

"He loves you," Scott stated, his gaze still troubled.

"Yes," she agreed. "And I love him, so I tolerate it."

"But you won't tolerate it from me?"

She grinned. "Not yet. We've only just met."

"Would you…" He had the sweetest look of indecision on his face that made Trista want to say yes to whatever he was going to ask just to put him out of his misery.

"Would you want to go to a movie with me tomorrow night?" he finished quickly

Warning bells went off in her head. She wanted to refuse, but her lips wouldn't let the words out. Wasn't she planning on going to the theater tomorrow anyway? "Are you asking me on a date?"

For a beat he looked stunned, then slowly shrugged.

"Is that allowed?"

His eyebrows pulled together. "What?"

"I mean, you're a pastor. Can you date?"

He chuckled. "Yes. I have a special dispensation." He winked.

"Oh." A date? With him? Not a good idea for so many reasons. "I'm not looking for a relationship," she stated firmly.

He looked relieved. "Neither am I."

So it wasn't a date. A burst of irritation surprised her.

"How about if we meet at the cinema," he continued. "Then it's just two new friends watching the same movie. Not a date."

Pushing aside her unsettling annoyance, she nodded, thankful he'd come up with a doable plan. "That would work. I'll meet you there for the last matinee. I think Ross and Kelly will watch Aidan for me. Could we go see that new thriller everyone has been talking about?"

He grinned. "That's funny. That's exactly what I was thinking."

A little shiver tripped down her spine. Was it co-incidence or were they really in tune with each other? She wasn't sure she wanted to know the answer to that question.

As Trista pushed Aidan in the stroller back to her apartment, she couldn't believe she'd agreed to meet a pastor at the movies. Ross was going to laugh until he cried. She'd just have to convince her big brother this was *not* a date.

Lynda Matthews pulled into the driveway of their large new mansion on the outskirts of town. She couldn't park in the garage because of her husband's many cars. Douglas collected vintage roadsters. Just one of many expensive passions.

Like the house. It was too big, showy and a bit garish. Lots of brick and columns and shiny accou-trements that screamed "look at me." She didn't like the place, but Douglas had insisted they buy the house when they relocated to town.

It was his money, as he loved to remind her, so she had no say in the matter.

"Come on, honey," she said to Logan. "Let's go

see if Kay has made something delicious for lunch."

The inside of the house was just as overdone as the outside. Cold marble flooring, a round marble table with an expensive vase filled with exotic flowers greeted them as they entered. Sometimes Lynda felt as if she were walking into a hotel rather than a home.

She took off her warm wool coat and then helped Logan out of his parka. She laid both on the table.

"Where have you been?"

Lynda froze at her husband's question. Then with a quick sweep of her hand, she pulled Logan behind her as she turned to face Douglas.

He stood in the doorway of the library off to her right. His six-foot-one frame filled the opening. He still wore the expensive navy suit he'd worn for his TV show *Afternoons with Douglas Matthews*. He was a handsome man with his jet-black hair and piercing blue eyes. The camera and his fans loved him. At one time, Lynda had, as well.

"We went to story time at the new bookstore downtown," she answered quietly.

He raised his eyebrows as anger sparked in his eyes. "You went out in public like that?" He made a sweeping gesture with his hand.

She stiffened, expecting him to berate her for

showing her face in public. Showing his shame in public.

"You know how important image is. You're my wife and I expect you to dress the part."

Of course, her clothing was his main concern. She'd thought her trendy yet conservative long skirt and blouse were very pretty.

"And it wouldn't have hurt to put a little more makeup on that eye," he added.

"I'm sorry. I should have thought it through better."

His expression relaxed slightly. "Yes, you should have. Logan, come out from behind your mother's skirt."

Logan tugged at her and Lynda's heart squeezed tight. She wanted to protect her son from Douglas's criticism, yet she knew if they defied him, criticism would be the least of her worries. She grasped Logan's hand, giving him a reassuring squeeze as she gently pulled him forward, but keeping him within arm's reach.

Douglas had never raised a hand to Logan, but Lynda still wanted Logan close enough that she could shield him if necessary.

Logan looked so much like his father. The same black hair and stunning eyes, but he had Lynda's disposition, much to Douglas's annoyance.

"Son, did you enjoy the story hour?"

Logan nodded.

"Speak up," Douglas snapped.

"Yes, sir, I did."

Douglas bestowed one of his charming smiles on his son. "Good. It is important to be seen in town at functions that promote learning."

Good for *your* image, Lynda thought but knew better than to put voice to her sarcasm.

"Will you be having lunch with us?" she asked.

He waved away her question. "No. I'm having lunch at the country club with Helene and Neal Harcourt. They've been big supporters of my show."

Relief swept over her like a cool breeze. "Very well then. We won't keep you. Come, Logan, let's find Kay."

As they went in search of the housekeeper-cook, Lynda could feel her husband's gaze on her back. She stuck her hand in the pocket of her skirt and fingered the edges of Trista Van Zandt's card.

Tomorrow she would call her.

That night at her brother's house, Trista watched with wry amusement as Ross laughed until his eyes watered.

"You're going...out with Pastor Scott?" Ross asked for the umpteenth time.

"We're not going 'out.' We're meeting at the movies. There'll be a big group of people there."

"Group?" Kelly exclaimed. "You joined The Kingdom Room, didn't you?"

Sheepishly, Trista nodded.

At Ross's questioning look, Kelly explained. "It's an online single friends group that Naomi started."

"I think that's great!" he managed to say between guffaws.

"Then why are you crying?" Trista asked, drily.

Kelly reached across Aidan to squeeze Trista's hand. "Don't mind him. We think it's great." Kelly gave Ross a pointed look before turning her gaze back to Trista. "Scott is a very nice man."

"Nice, as in wimp or nice, as in well mannered?" Trista teased.

Kelly grinned. "Definitely well mannered. I can't say about the other."

Trista shrugged. "It doesn't matter either way. This is just two friends seeing the same movie. It's not going anywhere."

Ross wiped at his eyes. "Never say never." He gazed adoringly at his wife.

Something akin to envy twisted in Trista's heart. Her brother and Kelly truly loved one another. Their union had come with a price, though.

Kelly's biological mother, Sandra Lange, had hired Ross as a private investigator to find the daughter she'd given up for adoption. Ross had found Kelly but also had uncovered a web of deceit that her biological father's wife had woven over the years. The fallout had been steep. Sandra had ended up in the hospital in a coma and Kelly's biological father, Gerald Morrow, then the mayor of Chestnut Grove, helped to bring his wife to justice.

"So, will you be able to watch Aidan for me?"

Ross sobered. "Yes, on one condition. You come to church with us in the morning and then go see Mom with me."

Trista gritted her teeth. "That's two conditions and no to both."

Ross got that determined, 'I'm going to have my way' look she hated. "Trista, it's not okay for you to turn your back on Mom."

"I'm not," she protested. But guilt and shame ran a ragged course through her. She hardened her heart to both. She would not feel bad for not wanting to see her mother. The woman hadn't been there for her growing up. Why should she be there for her now?

Trista stood and began to unbuckle Aidan from the high chair. "You know what? Forget it. I'll figure something else out."

Kelly reached for her hand. "Of course we'll watch him."

Ross came around the table to put his arms around Trista much as he had when they were kids. Love for her brother brought tears to her eyes. She'd burdened him her whole life with her problems, and she still was. He'd been the rock in her chaotic world. She clung to him.

"Sis, I just worry that Mom will pass on before you make peace with her."

She gave him a squeeze before disengaging from him. "I appreciate your concern. But I don't feel I need to make peace with her."

Ross sighed and nodded. "Well, would you at least come to church with us since you're dating the assistant pastor?"

Exasperated, she glared at him. "I'm *not* dating him."

His mouth twisted with suppressed mirth. "Whatever. Will you?"

"I'll think about it."

To Kelly, Ross stated, "That's her way of ending a discussion without committing. It usually means no."

Hefting a sleepy Aidan on her hip, Trista smiled. "Call me in the morning. That's as much as I can promise."

"Hey, that's something." Ross grinned.

Trista kissed her family goodbye and then drove to her apartment. By the time she arrived, Aidan was fast asleep. He didn't even stir when she changed his clothes and laid him in his crib.

As she was getting herself ready for bed, the phone rang.

"Hello?"

"Hi, babe."

She cringed. She should have let the machine pick up the call. "Kevin, what do you want?"

"Oh, are we in a bad mood?"

She closed her eyes as anger washed through her. "Kevin, it's late. Why are you calling?"

"I miss you."

She nearly gagged. "Right."

"Seriously." He sounded offended. "I'm coming to see you tomorrow."

Her heart stalled in her chest. "Why?"

"We need to talk."

"I think we've said everything we need to say."

"I'll be there around two."

She scrambled for an excuse. "We won't be here. Aidan and I are going with Ross to visit Mom."

There was a moment of silence before he said, "All right. I have an appointment on Monday so how about Tuesday. I'll take you to lunch."

"I'll have to check my schedule and let you know if that will work."

"Fine. I'll call you tomorrow night to confirm." He hung up without another word.

Trista sat there staring at the phone as if it was a snake about to bite her. She hated that Kevin thought he could just invade her life whenever he wanted. The man had walked out on her and their one-month-old child, stating he wasn't ready to be a father. She had had so much hope that he'd have a change of heart. He hadn't. And it wasn't until after he'd left that she found out about the other woman. Her life had become a cliché.

Agitated by Kevin's call and knowing it was too late at night to call the lawyer who'd handled her divorce, Trista fired up her laptop and entered The Kingdom Room, but joining the discussion going on in the chat room didn't appeal.

But she needed to talk with someone. She opened her e-mail and sent a post to *Called2serve*.

She was surprised when a reply popped almost immediately into her in-box.

Momof1
This must be confusing and painful for you. I can only say that people do change and everyone deserves a second chance. If you don't feel com-

fortable talking to him alone, find a friend, a family member or a pastor who would mediate for you. This might be a good opportunity for you to draw closer to God.

Called2serve

Trista didn't want to give Kevin another chance. He'd hurt her horribly. But she knew she had to hear what he had to say. He was, after all, Aidan's father, even if he didn't want to be.

She couldn't ask Ross to meet Kevin with her. He'd just as soon pummel Kevin than mediate between them. Nor would she ask Kelly in her condition. Trista thought about maybe one of the Bensons, but she really didn't want to drag her new bosses into her old life. She'd call her lawyer for advice on Monday but she could already guess what she'd say, "No, don't do it."

The only other person Trista could think of asking was the man she'd be seeing on a nondate tomorrow.

Pastor Scott was probably going to regret ever wanting to be her friend.

Chapter Four

Trista tried to keep her stomach from roiling at the nauseating smell of antiseptics mixed with… She shuddered. The underlying scent of body fluids, decay and death clung to the air. Trista dug her fingers into the palms of her hands. She didn't want to be here.

If she hadn't told Kevin she was coming and hadn't been fully awake this morning when Ross called to see if she'd changed her mind about visiting Mom, she'd be home playing with her son.

An older woman approached Trista and Ross when they entered the assisted living facility where their mother now lived. "Mr. Van Zandt. It's good to see you."

Ross shook the woman's hand. "Hello, Mrs. Angelo. This is my sister, Trista."

Mrs. Angelo turned her high-wattage smile to Trista. Her graying hair curled at the edges of her round face. "We've met. It's been a while."

Trista didn't take offense at the woman's subtle reprimand. The woman didn't understand the history of Trista's relationship with her mother so of course Mrs. Angelo would think it odd that a daughter wouldn't want to see her own mother.

But feelings of anger and resentment were the only emotions Trista associated with her mother. Emotions Trista would just as soon not feel. "Yes, it has," she managed to reply.

"How is my mother today?" Ross asked as they moved away from the administration desk down the hall toward their mother's room.

"She's slowing down and has had some bad days recently," Mrs. Angelo stated.

In self-preservation, Trista tuned their conversation out and grudgingly tagged along at Ross's heels. A position, she noted with irony, she'd deliberately taken most of her life because of the measure of safety and comfort it gave her. And did even now.

Keeping her gaze averted from the other resident's open doors, she silently recited her childhood mantra, *This too shall pass. This too shall pass.*

She just wanted to get this visit over as quickly and as painlessly as possible without being swamped with the anger and hurt that so often threatened to choke her whenever she let memories of her childhood flood her mind.

They entered her mother's room. The small space was decorated with a cozy recliner, fresh flowers in several vases and gleaming CD boxes sitting on an antique sideboard. All Kelly's doing, Trista knew.

On the wall hung pictures of peaceful meadows and sparkling brooks. The metal-frame bed was empty with the side railing down.

"Michelle?" Mrs. Angelo called, her voice merry with just a hint of anxiety in it.

Trista watched Ross check the adjoining bathroom. He came out and shook his head. "Could she be outside?" he asked.

Mrs. Angelo frowned. "I suppose. Why don't we check the garden? She loves to sit near the pond with the ducks."

"I'll go," Trista volunteered. Anything to get out of this building.

A noise from the closet drew their attention. Ross opened the closet door. Her mother sat curled into a ball tucked against the back of the closet. Her graying hair hung in tangled clumps and her dark eyes were unfocused. Her pink flowered nightclothes were bunched up around her knees.

Trista sucked in a breath. Her heart caved in on itself.

"Mom? What are you doing?" Ross asked as he bent down to see her.

Michelle ducked her head and curled tighter.

A sense of surrealism stole over Trista. Why was her mother cowering from Ross? She'd never seen her mother like this. She didn't want to see her mom as anything other than the awful woman who'd given birth to her.

"What's wrong with her?" Trista asked, her voice shaky.

Mrs. Angelo moved forward. "She's been having flashbacks. It happens with advancing Alzheimer's." She squatted down beside Ross. "Michelle? Honey, you're safe. Come out now."

Mom shook her head.

"Are you hungry? I have some cookies," Mrs. Angelo coaxed.

Michelle held out her hand. Mrs. Angelo dug into the pocket of her white coat and brought out a small wrapped cookie. After removing the wrapper, she held the cookie just out of Michelle's reach.

Slowly, Michelle uncurled and crawled out.

Ross reached to help her but she flinched away. She allowed Mrs. Angelo to help her to her feet and grabbed the cookie.

Trista held her hand to her mouth as horror clawed at her throat. Pity and empathy washed over her, making her angry. She didn't want to feel anything for this woman.

Ross's eyes were sad as he stood. Trista stared at him. Why had he made her come here?

Mrs. Angelo helped Michelle shuffle to the bed. Watching how slow and fragile her mother had become cut Trista to the bone.

She hated caring, but wouldn't have wished this on her worst enemy.

Mrs. Angelo tucked Michelle into the bed and lifted the railing, locking it into place. "You have visitors, Michelle. Your son and your daughter are here. They want to see you. Isn't that nice?"

Michelle seemed to sink into the bedding. Trista half expected her to disappear. She looked so frail and vulnerable, so unlike the woman Trista remembered. This woman wasting away in front of her couldn't be her mother, the one who had been loud, sarcastic and always smelled of alcohol.

Ross pulled up a folding chair. "Trista?"

She shook her head, declining the offer to sit closer. She just couldn't.

"I'll leave you all alone. Just ring if you need me," Mrs. Angelo said before shutting the door behind her.

Ross spoke softly to their mother. Her eyes watched him and recognition slowly entered her expression.

"Kelly's healthy and so is the baby. We only have a month to go. We'll bring the little one in as soon as we can. Kelly wanted to come today, but she had some work to do at the adoption agency and she's watching Aidan."

Michelle nodded, her gaze shifting. "Who's that over there?"

Trista's heart withered a bit even though she'd been through this the last time she'd visited. Knowing it was the quickest way to get this over with, she stepped forward. "It's me, Mom. Trista."

Mom seemed to absorb that. "Okay. How's my grandson?"

Surprise and pleasure arced through her. "Aidan's good, Mom. Real good."

Mom turned her attention back to Ross. "I found some pictures the other day." She waved a hand at Trista. "Hand me that binder over there, would you?" She pointed to the sideboard.

The bossy, autocratic Michelle shone through for the moment. Feeling calmer and on more familiar ground, Trista picked up the leather-bound photo album. She'd never seen this. She looked at Ross. He shrugged, obviously sharing her bewilderment. Trista handed the book over.

Mom opened the heavy cover to reveal a picture of a couple on their wedding day. Trista leaned in closer to study the black-and-white photo with faded edges showing a white chapel with stained glass windows in the background.

A tuxedoed man and his bride in her finery smiled for the camera. The bride had dark hair caught up on top with a beautiful headpiece that cascaded down in the back. The slim-fitting dress spoke of a different era.

"Who's that?" Trista asked.

Mom quickly turned the page. "Just my parents."

The harshness of her mother's tone stunned Trista. She exchanged a quick glance with Ross, who seemed just as taken aback.

Their mother had never talked much about her family. Trista knew that her grandparents had been killed in a boating accident before Trista was born.

The next few pages showed Michelle as a child. She was a cute little girl with dark pigtails and a huge smile.

From the looks of the pictures she seemed to

have had a happy childhood and Trista said as much.

"What do you know about it?" Mom barked.

"You look happy in this picture, Mom," Ross interjected and pointed to a picture of Michelle and her father.

"Yeah, well, looks can be deceiving." She slammed the book closed.

Trista frowned. She'd never thought much about her mother's childhood. Michelle hadn't been the warm and fuzzy type of mother. She hadn't shared stories of her girlhood or had even taken much of an interest in Trista's girlhood.

A disappointment that still stung.

But now that she had her own child, she did wonder what had happened to make her mother so cold.

Taking the book, Trista sat in the recliner. Flipping through the photos kept her from having to relate to her mother. Though she wasn't sure how she felt about glimpsing into her mother's life. There were pictures of birthday parties and friends. Michelle as a child, a preteen. Then as a teen.

As the pictures progressed in age, Trista noticed a marked difference in the way her mother looked. The smile had dimmed to the point where as a teen she looked sullen. The sparkle in her eyes had disappeared.

In the earlier pictures, Michelle had looked so happy, especially in the photos with her father, a tall, good-looking man with a charming smile.

Trista paused and folded back a picture of a teenage Michelle and her father to compare with an earlier photo. In the first image, father and daughter were laughing and she was leaning into him. In the later picture, her father had his arm around Michelle, holding her in place as if she might bolt at any moment.

But it was the expression in her eyes that disturbed Trista. She'd seen that sort of haunted, battered expression before.

Recently, in fact.

On Lynda Matthews.

A chill ran over Trista's skin. Had her grandfather abused her mother? Was that why she'd become an alcoholic? Why she hadn't taken much interest in her children?

Swallowing back the lump of compassion lodged in her throat, Trista stood. "We should go."

Ross frowned and shook his head. "Not yet."

"Go?" Michelle asked. Her thin hand clutched at the bed railing. "I want to go. Please don't leave me here."

Ross shot Trista a glare before patting Mom's hand. "This is where you live now, Mom. You're fine. Everything is fine."

Michelle sat up and stared at Trista. "Mother, is that you?"

Forcing back the sudden tears that sprang to the backs of her eyes, Trista said, "It's me, Trista."

Michelle tried to get up. "I need to find my mother before he comes home. I don't want to be alone with him."

A sickening dread filled Trista. She wanted to leave but she was drawn forward with a morbid sense of curiosity and the need to help her mother. "Who don't you want to be alone with?"

"Mom, settle down," Ross directed as he tried to ease Michelle back.

"No, don't hurt me!" Michelle shouted as she fought against him.

He pushed the call button.

Trista grabbed her mother's hand. The bones felt so small and crushable. "Who hurt you? Was it your father?"

Michelle pulled her hand away with surprising strength. An ugly rage lit the depths of her dark eyes. "I'll never let him do that again. I'll never let anyone hurt me again."

"Oh, Mom." Trista's heart twisted in her chest

and the need to protect rose sharply, unexpect-edly. "No one's going to hurt you. You're safe here."

Mrs. Angelo rushed in the room, took one look at the situation and turned back around. A moment later she returned followed by an orderly. "Okay, visiting time is over." In her hand she held a hy-podermic needle.

"What are you giving her?" Trista demanded.

"Just a little valium. Nothing that will harm her," she answered as she tried to maneuver her way past Trista.

Ross took Trista by the shoulders and moved her back. "Let her do her job."

The orderly held Mom down as Mrs. Angelo gave her the shot. Within a few moments the orderly was able to let go and Mom once again sank back into the bedding. She closed her eyes and her breathing eased.

Trista stopped Mrs. Angelo in the hallway. "I think she was abused by her father. Do you know anything about that?"

Mrs. Angelo's expression became sympathetic. "I gathered that from things she has said over the past few months. It's typical for patients with Alzheimer's to relive painful memories, especially if they've never dealt with them."

Trista turned her gaze to Ross. "We have to do something. To help her."

Ross's big brown eyes showed sorrow. "We're doing what we can."

"I can give you some literature on the disease," offered Mrs. Angelo.

A deep welling of pity and compassion robbed Trista of her voice. Not only was her mother suffering from this awful disease but the past abuse was tormenting her mind.

Trista nodded, indicating she'd take the literature. When Mrs. Angelo came back with some pamphlets, Trista stuffed them in her purse and allowed Ross to lead her to the car.

A strange numbness seeped into Trista. Sitting in the passenger seat watching life go by outside kept her from thinking about her mother. About the trauma she'd revealed.

"You okay?" Ross asked.

"Did you know?" Trista twisted in the seat to stare at his strong profile.

His jaw clenched, then slowly he nodded.

"When?"

"Dad told me years ago."

His words hit her like a fist to the gut. "Years ago? Why didn't you tell me?"

"You were fifteen and angry at the world."

She clenched her fists. "I wasn't angry at the world. I was angry with them. You should have told me."

"And what would you have done with that knowledge?"

"I don't know. It would have helped me understand her. Maybe I could have convinced her to get help."

He gave her a sharp glance. "Don't you think Dad tried?"

"He was a drunk, too. How could he help her?"

How many times had she seen Ross drag their dad home from a drinking binge? How many times had she witnessed her mother and father sharing a bottle? Too many to count and too many to forget.

"He didn't always drink. You were too young to remember, but he was a good dad in the beginning. For both of us. But years with Mom and her repressed anger and hate beat him down. I think it was easier for him to join her in drinking than trying to fight her to stop."

"That sucks," Trista fumed.

"Yes, it does. But it's the reality we have."

"I wish you had told me. If not then, at least later. Before I married Kevin."

"What does Kevin have to do with this?"

Trista shrugged, unwilling to reveal that Kevin

wanted to meet with her and how upsetting she found that. "I might have done things differently. I might have tried to forge a relationship with Mother before she got like this."

Regret and sadness clutched at her making her ache.

"Well, I can't change the past."

"I know." She sighed and pulled out the pamphlets on Alzheimer's. "Why do you think she never got counseling?"

"Too ashamed. Too full of pride. I don't know."

The need to understand burned in her chest. "I want to find out what happened to her. Did he beat her? Sexually assault her? Did her mother know?"

"You'll make yourself crazy asking questions like that. She's not in any shape to tell you and you'd only upset her if you try to make her." His expression was tender when he glanced over at her. "Leave it alone, Trista. Concentrate on your life. Yours and Aidan's."

But that was just it. She needed to understand her mother's past so she could be a better mother to Aidan. An image of Lynda rose in her mind. The bruise, the scared expression in her son's eyes. Trista had to find a way to help Lynda, especially since it was too late to help her mother.

Ross pulled up outside of Trista's apartment. "So what time is your date with Pastor Scott?"

She'd forgotten about that. She poked Ross in the ribs. "It's not a date." She glanced at her watch. "And I'm going to be late if I don't hurry and freshen up." She slid out of the car. "I'll call Kelly and let her know you're on your way home."

He grinned. "I'm sure Aidan's just fine."

Wrinkling up her nose, she stated, "I'm sure he is, too."

She waved goodbye and then went to her apartment. It was cold and empty. Unbearable without Aidan.

After calling Kelly, she changed out of her linen pantsuit and into jeans and a sweater. Just as she was rushing to the door the phone rang. Thinking it might be Kelly calling back, she answered.

"Hello?"

"Hey, babe."

She frowned as irritation heated her skin. "You said you'd call tomorrow."

"I had a moment. So how about lunch on Tuesday?"

"I told you I'd have to check my schedule at work. Call me tomorrow evening."

"Right. The big lawyerly schedule."

Her blood pressure rose at the dig. "What is it you need to speak to me about, anyway?"

"I want to reconnect with my favorite girl," he replied smoothly.

"Favorite until the next one comes along," she shot back.

"Come on, no need to get nasty. I'd like to talk. Nothing more. I'll call you tomorrow." He hung up.

Trista slammed down the receiver and sank onto the couch. The emotional roller coaster the day had turned out to be was wearing her down. All she wanted to do was curl up next to Aidan and sleep.

But how did she get hold of the pastor to cancel their…not-a-date date?

Scott stood in line outside the Chestnut Grove theater with a ticket in his hand. He'd wanted to buy Trista's ticket, but he was afraid she wouldn't appreciate it since this was not a date.

The late-afternoon sun turned the snow on the ground to slush. People were taking advantage of the break in the blustery fall weather. The long line outside the theater began to move and Scott stepped forward, his gaze searching the street for any sign of Trista.

He checked his watch. The movie was set to start in ten minutes. She was already a half hour late. A disquieting queasiness roused old fears and insecurities. Was Trista standing him up?

He checked his e-mail on his PDA. No new mail.

At the door to the theater, he stepped out of line and moved closer to the ticket box. He could turn in his ticket and get a refund. Disappointment and irritation settled heavily on his chest. He'd been looking forward to getting to know Trista.

"I'd like a refund please," he told the cashier behind the glass.

The young boy looked bored. "I'm sorry. We don't give refunds once the show has begun."

He frowned as annoyance tightened in his chest. "There's still five minutes."

The boy shrugged, unconcerned. "The previews have started. Sorry. Theater policy."

"Scott?"

At the sound of Trista's voice something in Scott lightened. He turned to see her hurrying toward him. She looked sleek and beautiful in her faded jeans, dark boots and red sweater beneath an unzipped black parka. Her hair hung loose and blew crazily in the late-afternoon breeze.

"Is it too late?" she asked between breaths.

"I don't know." Scott turned back to the boy. "Can I buy another ticket?"

"Sorry. It's sold out."

"Bummer," Trista said. "I'm sorry."

Relief that she hadn't stood him up made him smile. "No problem."

He studied her face. There were black smudges beneath her eyes. From the cold or from tears? His chest knotted with concern and his earlier irritation dissipated. "How about a cup of hot chocolate and piece of pie instead?"

"That sounds wonderful."

"Good. I'm not sure I'm up for the Starlight Diner. How about the bookstore café?"

"Perfect. And I'm game to walk to the café if you are," she said.

"Let's," he agreed and held out his arm.

As they walked down Main Street to The Reading Rainbow Palace, Scott sensed the pensive mood overtaking Trista. He hoped she'd trust him enough to open up about what was bothering her because he'd like to help her.

And he couldn't deny how nice it felt to have her on his arm. But this was not a date.

Chapter Five

"This rivals the Starlight any day," Trista said between bites of Dutch apple pie. The toasted brown sugar melted in her mouth and the spices, cinnamon and nutmeg, combined with the tart apples were nirvana for her taste buds.

Scott grinned. "I think this came from the Starlight."

She liked the way the corners of his eyes crinkled. "Really?" She shook her head. "They outdid themselves then."

"Considering I wolfed mine down in three bites, I'd say so," he agreed.

"Well, it's not like you have to watch your weight." She'd more than noticed his trim physique, his broad shoulders and all-American good looks. Dressed in cargo pants and a rugby shirt under his leather bomber, he looked more like a model in a magazine than a pastor. Which made this "not a date" not only harder, but confusing.

"So, Ross mentioned this morning that you two were going to visit your mother. How did that go?"

She met his gaze, noting the darker blue ring around the lighter blue irises. "You talked to Ross?"

"After church."

Uh-oh. She braced herself, wondering if her brother had grilled him about meeting her at the movie. "What did he say?"

"Just what I told you. Should he have said something more?"

"No," she said.

"You didn't answer my question."

Stalling, she took a sip of her cocoa.

"I'm guessing it didn't go so well?"

When the moment stretched, she relented because she had no reason to be rude. "It was...how much has Ross told you about our mother?"

His gaze turned sympathetic. "A little. She has Alzheimer's."

Trista laid down her fork. Tension pulled at the muscles in her shoulders. Still she hesitated, uncomfortable with the chaos of emotions the visit had brought. She reminded herself he was a pastor, a man who should be good at listening and giving advice. And she had a favor to ask of him—as a pastor. "Mom's in the advanced stages. She thought I was her mother."

"That must be hard for you to see her in that condition."

Pressing her lips together to keep her emotions under control, Trista nodded. "We found her in the closet, hiding. Her nurse said it's typical of Alzheimer's victims to relive some trauma from the past. I think she was abused by her father as a child."

"I'm so sorry."

"I guess it makes sense. Some abused children grow to abuse their own children." Seeing the leap of concern in the pastor's eyes, she quickly added, "Ross and I were never physically hurt." She frowned as some memory just beyond her reach tapped for attention. "At least I don't think we were. But my mother was emotionally abusive. I sometimes can still hear her voice in my head telling me I'm no good, I won't amount to anything."

He reached out to lay a hand over hers. "And look what you've done with your life. You've succeeded. You didn't let your mother's words dictate your future," he pointed out.

Taking comfort from his touch, she said, "That was more Ross's influence than anything else. He was the anchor in the storm of my childhood."

"What about your father?"

A vague image rose of her father sitting on the stoop of their flat in Brooklyn, his head resting on the iron railing, a bottle in a brown bag clutched in his hand. He smelled like booze and needed a shave. She'd skirt around him as she would a homeless man. She shrugged. "A drunk. He was such a nonentity for me. Just someone in the background of my life."

"Did you or Ross ever seek help?"

"Who would we have asked? Both sets of grandparents were gone. We didn't go church. No one at school cared."

"You two must have felt so alone. Scared."

She appreciated his empathy but she didn't want his pity. She'd had enough of that from her in-laws to last a lifetime. "We managed. Like you said, we succeeded in spite of our parents. But now I'm a mom. I want to understand the past so I don't make mistakes that hurt Aidan."

He squeezed her hand. "You're a good mother. You won't repeat the past."

On some level she knew he was right. "But I have made some mistakes, used bad judgment, and I know that the way I grew up contributed to those decisions. I want to understand my mother but I don't know how to deal with her."

"You don't have to deal with her alone," he said, his voice gentle.

Trista linked her fingers around his. Hanging on to the feelings of trust and support he offered. "Thank you. I appreciate how easy you are to talk to."

His smile was pensive. "I'm glad you think so. But I meant let God comfort you. Give Him the past and trust Him with your future."

His words brought an ache to her chest. "That sounds so much easier than I know it is." She held his warm brown gaze, seeing the tenderness of his soul. "I haven't let God into my life," she confessed. "Growing up as I did, I couldn't see how God cared." She still didn't.

"I understand. Without someone to guide you to the truth, how could you find it?"

His words, full of sincerity, touched her heart. He wasn't placating her. He wasn't feeding her a line. Somehow she knew that. And that made her want to know more about him. "Who guided you to God?"

His eyes lit up. "My grandfather. He used to sit me on his knee and talk about God."

She envied him such a memory. "So your family was religious."

"Not really." The light in his eyes dimmed. "My parents are very pragmatic and they raised three out of four kids to be just like them. Can't see it, don't believe it. I'm the black sheep."

"What? The black sheep? Because you're a pastor?"

He nodded. "My parents are both highly successful doctors, my two brothers are highly successful lawyers and my sister is a highly successful pediatrician. Overachievers all. And then there's me."

He gave a self-effacing wince. "I've never received the best grades, never was president of any clubs in high school or college, and was never, ever interested in business or science or math or biology. I can't even balance my check book."

"I'm sure they're proud of you," she stated. "How could anyone not be proud of you?"

"Oh, I like you." He grinned. "You feed my ego."

She grinned back. "It's good you had your grandfather, then."

"Definitely. We all need someone in our lives to show us the way."

Terri Reed   89

She didn't have anyone to show her the way. Until now. "I have you," she quipped.

His grin brought a warm flush to her cheeks.

There had been a reason she'd wanted to talk with Scott. She better ask him now before she lost her nerve. "I have a favor to ask of you."

"Go ahead."

Her heartbeat picked up. What if he said no? The thought of facing Kevin alone squeezed her chest with dread; she had to risk asking for Scott's help for Aidan's sake. "I've agreed to meet with my ex-husband on Tuesday and I really don't want to meet him alone."

Scott blinked.

She rushed on. "I was hoping you'd agree to meet with us. Sort of mediate. I don't know what he wants, but I know from experience that he can twist my mind around his little finger. I can't let that happen anymore," she added fiercely.

Releasing her hand, Scott sat back, creating a distance that Trista felt keenly and sent regret sliding through her. But it couldn't be helped.

"Of course. I would be glad to. Why don't we meet at the church? We have a counseling room that would work perfectly."

"The church," she squeaked.

"Is that a problem?"

"No. Umm…I don't think so." She hadn't set foot in a church since her wedding. Kevin's family had insisted on a huge ceremony in the largest church in Richmond, which they never let her forget they'd paid for. Even then, she'd felt uncomfortable and unwanted in the grand sanctuary. Certainly a sign that her marriage was doomed. "I'm sure Kevin won't have a problem with meeting there."

"Good." He stood. "Are you done?" he asked, indicating the plate in front of her.

She nodded and watched as he took the remnants of their dessert to the counter. When he came back, he didn't sit down. Feeling his withdrawal like a deep ache in her bones, she rose and he helped her with her coat. His breath was warm on her cheek as he adjusted her collar. For a moment the urge to turn and meet his lips with her own captured her.

"Thank you," she managed to murmur as she stepped back, realizing that though she was relieved and grateful for his calming presence and his willingness to mediate between her and Kevin, she was having a hard time not seeing him as an attractive man whom she'd like to get closer to.

How insane was that?

Trista rocked Aidan to sleep, loving the downy softness of his cheek against her neck and the gentle snoring in her ear. This was her favorite time of night, when she and Aidan were in their apartment, the lights down low and she could hold him without him squirming to play.

She pushed the floor with her toe and sent the rocker into motion. Despite the peace and comfort of home and Aidan, her thoughts were racing around her head like a pinball let loose.

The visit to her mother had shaken her to the core. It made her mad that Ross had kept her in the dark about her mom's past for so long. She could only hope that she'd be able to discover more about her mother before she passed away. Ross might not think it would be productive, but Trista couldn't let the idea go.

That she had told Scott about the visit and her suspicions hadn't been planned. But the relief of having someone to share the burden with was very welcome.

As was having his promised presence when she met with Kevin.

Only…she cringed inwardly, thinking about having to reveal the details of her failed marriage to Scott. A deep sense of shame washed over her, tightening her chest. She'd naively thought she'd have a better life than she'd had with her parents when she married Kevin. What a joke.

His parents had never accepted her and Kevin had held his family's wealth over her head as if she should be grateful that he'd lowered himself to marry her.

Now she was a divorced single mother. Even in the modern world, there was a stigma attached to her like some neon sign. Scott hadn't seemed bothered by the fact she was divorced and a mom. But being nonjudgmental was part of being a pastor, right?

What did the man underneath think?

And why did she care?

Because somewhere deep inside lurked the naive romantic who longed for the happily-ever-after with a man like Scott.

A mocking voice in her head laughed. Get a grip!

There was no way a pastor would ever have a relationship with a damaged, divorced, single mom.

Her shoulders slumped and she hugged Aidan tighter as tears gathered in her throat.

Scott was just a nice guy, doing what he thought God wanted of him. She would have to keep a tight rein on her attraction to him, because no way was she up for more hurt.

Scott stared out the window of his church office at the snow falling gently, obscuring the yellow parking lines of the parking lot with white dust. His thoughts were just as obscure.

After escorting Trista back to her car last night, he'd walked around trying to sort through his chaotic thoughts. With no luck. He'd finally settled on seeing the late movie that he and Trista had missed as a way to occupy his mind. But it hadn't really helped.

He kept going over the conversation with Trista. He'd been flattered she'd talked to him about her mother's situation. And he'd been unnerved that he'd talked about his family. He rarely did.

He ached in his soul that she'd witnessed her mother in such a declining state and he wished he could help her come to terms with her mother's illness.

Leading her to God's love would take time. Showing her how to find comfort and peace in the middle of a difficult period should be easy.

Except, his attraction for her clouded the situation. He really liked her, enjoyed her company and found he could watch her and never grow tired. He didn't know if he could be objective and patient enough to guide her.

And he really didn't know what to make of her request to mediate with her ex-husband.

She'd called earlier to schedule the time. He

penciled it in to his calendar. Writing her name and her ex-husband's name down had knotted his chest with something close to dread, because he knew that his job as a pastor and a man of God would be to advocate for their marriage, even though it was legally over.

No matter how he felt about her. Maybe this was all some kind of test.

There were so many reasons why he couldn't pursue a relationship with Trista. She was a non-believer, divorced, a mom and struggling with issues that he didn't know if he wanted to deal with.

Needing some distraction, he spun around to his computer and fired up his Internet browser. He logged on to The Kingdom Room and joined the thread of discussion about the movie.

He posted his thoughts on the premise and the actor's portrayals of the characters.

Coming across an answer to a question that intrigued him, he scrolled back through the post looking for the original question. He found a post by *Momof1* in which she'd stated she'd been too busy over the weekend to see the movie, but was enjoying hearing everyone's take on the film.

Scott finally found the question, which to his surprise also came from *Momof1*. She asked if there were any Christian themes running through the movie that she could watch for when she got the chance to see it.

He took a moment to contemplate the question and asked God to reveal any subtle messages in the movie to him. Later, he sent a post.

Hi all,

Momof1 asked if there were any Christian themes running through the movie. I found the lead character facing his fear in order to protect and save those he loved a reflection of Jesus' actions on the cross. If you read Matthew 26:39, Jesus expresses His fear of the suffering to come. But He, who could have saved Himself with His supernatural powers, relinquished His power and His life to protect and save God's people.

Called2serve

That was him. Called to serve. And he'd serve Trista as best he could and keep emotionally detached, no matter what.

And pray that he'd be able to keep such a vow.

Ross Van Zandt sat at the small desk in the extra office that Kelly asked him to use at Tiny Blessings. The window above his head let in some natural light to mingle with the overhead light. A stack of yellowed file folders sat in front of him. This most recent batch had been found in the wall of the Harcourt mansion when Reverend Fraser's son, Jonah, had been doing renovations. When would the madness end?

For two years, Ross had been working pro bono with Kelly to unravel the confusion over hundreds of adoption records that had been falsified by the agency's previous director, Barnaby Harcourt. All of the children who had been adopted through these underhanded means were now adults, several of whom wanted to find their biological parents.

There were some who didn't, and in many case files, the information was incomplete or plain wrong, making some of the adoptions illegal. Sorting through the truths and the lies was proving a dangerous endeavor.

Someone wanted all of this information to go away. Why else would they have broken into the adoption agency and set the place on fire?

Thankfully, Ross had been backing up his files daily so they hadn't lost everything on the computers, and these files had been safe at his house.

His SUV unfortunately, hadn't fared as well. Someone had smashed in the windshield and left a note warning him to drop his investigation.

Right. When pigs flew!

Tiny Blessings Adoption Agency meant the world to Kelly. And for her sake, Ross was committed to cleaning up the mess that Barnaby had made and building a good reputation for the agency.

Picking up the top file, Ross flipped it open, cross-referenced the information on the documents with the original files that corresponded.

The phone on the desk buzzed, indicating the receptionist was on the line.

"Yes?"

"Detective Fletcher to see you."

"Send him in." Ross closed the file and stood.

A moment later his office door opened and Zach Fletcher—six feet of muscle, brown wavy hair and intelligent, watchful blue eyes—entered. Ross considered Zach a man worth his salt.

They shook hands.

"Is this a social call or business?" Ross asked as he resumed his seat and indicated for Zach to take the chair on the other side of the desk.

Zach smiled. "A little of both. I came in to take Pilar to lunch, but she's not ready yet. I thought I'd compare notes on our investigations."

Pilar Estes, now Fletcher, had worked at Tiny Blessings since Kelly took it over after Barnaby

Harcourt was murdered. Pilar and Zach met when Pilar found a baby left on the doorstep of Tiny Blessings. Zach was able to reunite the baby with its mother and in the process Pilar and Zach fell in love. They were married not long after and had a child of their own, along with two adopted children.

"I'm slowly working my way through these records. Other than finally discovering Ben Cavanaugh's biological mother, I haven't found anything noteworthy."

"That's just as well," Zach stated.

"How's that?"

With a shrug, Zach said, "We have no new leads on the break-in or the notes. The perp could be any number of people who might not want something revealed. Off the record, as your friend, it might be a good idea to hold off on any more investigating."

Ross's hackles rose. "Excuse me? You're warning me off?"

Zach held up a hand. "It might be good to leave well enough alone. You stir a hornet's nest, you're bound to get stung."

"You know I can't hold off. The reputation of Tiny Blessings is at stake."

"I'm just saying, be careful. Run anything you find by me. Let me—"

A knock on the door interrupted Zach.

"Sorry," Ross murmured to Zach before calling out, "Yes?"

The door opened and Kelly, closely followed by Zach's wife, Pilar, strolled in. Both men rose as their wives came to their side. Though just barely reaching her husband's shoulder, Pilar had a strong presence. Her black curly hair, extremely dark eyes, and high cheekbones attested to her Puerto Rican heritage. Zach slipped his arm around Pilar's waist and kissed her cheek.

Kelly, though nearly at the end of her pregnancy, had a glow to her sweet face. Pride and love filled Ross's chest to bursting. He loved his wife with a deep passion that sometimes scared him. "Hey, gorgeous." He smiled and leaned close to touch his lips to hers in a quick kiss.

Pilar patted Zach's chest. "I'm ready for lunch when you are."

Ross met Zach's gaze. "We good?"

Zach gave a curt nod. "Yes. Just think about what I said."

"Knock, knock." Eric Pellegrino stood in the open doorway. Taller than even Zach, Eric had an energetic way about him that made people smile. His warm brown eyes crinkled at the corners. "So this is where the party's at."

Kelly had hired Eric so that she could spend more time with Ross, and soon, the baby. Eric's overseas work as a missionary in Africa and Thailand made him an asset to the agency.

"No party would be complete without you," quipped Pilar with a grin.

"Actually, we were just heading out to lunch," Zach said.

"Cool." To Pilar, he said, "When you come back, I need you to sign off on a file before I put it to bed."

"I can do it now," Pilar said and moved toward the door.

Eric held up his hand. "Later's fine."

"All right." Pilar took Zach's hand and with a wave they left.

"So what was that about?" Kelly asked as soon as she heard the front door close behind the Fletchers.

"Come in, Eric, and close the door," Ross instructed as he indicated for Kelly to take his desk chair.

She didn't hesitate. At this stage in the pregnancy, sitting was much preferred over standing. Easing into the leather captain's chair, she slipped off her shoes and made herself comfortable.

Eric took the seat Zach had occupied. He exchanged a curious glance with Kelly, at which she shrugged. Something had been going on between Ross and Zach when she'd walked in and Ross would tell her in his own time.

Ross crossed his arms over his chest. "Zach wanted to warn me off from going through these files."

Confused, Kelly shook her head. "Why? He's been so supportive."

"Do the police have any more leads on the break-in and the notes?" Eric asked.

Ross gave a negative shake of his head. "But Zach seems to believe that whoever is responsible doesn't want something in these files revealed."

"Well, that's obvious," Kelly remarked drily. The threatening notes, the break-in and the damage done to Ross's car made her nervous.

But she and Ross were both committed to clearing Tiny Blessings' reputation.

"It is." Ross's voice took on a deep intensity. "So, I need you both to promise to be very careful, and to report anything strange or out of the ordinary to me pronto. And don't take anything for granted. We don't know who's behind the recent events. It could very well be someone we know."

An ominous shiver of dread snaked its way down Kelly's spine.

Chapter Six

Late Monday afternoon, Trista sat in the movie theater. Using some vacation time to leave work early to catch a matinee had been the smartest thing she'd done in a long time. The discussion on The Kingdom Room site intrigued her, especially *Called2serve's* post. And the movie hadn't disappointed.

Watching the film with the perspective of God's sacrifice for His creations had made a rather tedious action flick so much more engaging.

That night after putting Aidan down, she sent a post.

Called2serve
  Hi, I just wanted to tell you how much the analogy of God's sacrifice helped make the movie

enjoyable. I'm usually not much for this type of movie.

Momof1

She hadn't expected *Called2serve* to reply until the next day so when a post came in a few minutes later, she was surprised and pleased. It was odd how the anonymity of conversing with someone on the Internet could be so satisfying and yet so scary. It was like having a pen pal, only in real time.

Momof1

Glad to hear you enjoyed the movie. I hadn't been to see a film in a long time, but going the other day reminded me of how much exposure the media has. And I hope to see more films that convey the message of hope that God brings. I was at the bookstore not long ago and noticed that the Christian fiction section was bigger than in the past. I think storytelling in all media is a great way to reach out to people. I picked up a suspense thriller and am really enjoying it. Have you read any good books lately?

Called2serve

For over an hour they "talked." The conversation went from books to the Bible to art and literature and then on to sports. They had a lot in common regarding their tastes in painters, writers and their loyalty to the Boston Red Sox.

Just as the conversation veered to politics, Aidan stirred in the other room. Trista signed off with the promise of "getting together" the next night.

After settling Aidan back down, Trista went to her room and readied herself for bed. But as she lay in her double bed alone, her thoughts became anxious about the upcoming meeting with Kevin. What did he want? After almost five months why would he want to talk?

She was so grateful that Scott had agreed to mediate. She trusted him and knew without a doubt that he would help her to keep perspective on the situation.

Only—she grimaced—she hadn't told him all the gory details of her marriage. Of Kevin's infidelity, of his controlling nature and the way she'd almost lost her identity to him over the years. Having Aidan was the only good point of that chapter in her life and her son had given her back her individuality.

She could only hope…she smiled in the dark, thinking that Scott would suggest she pray. Staring at the ceiling she quietly said, "God, I hope and pray that whatever happens tomorrow…"

She didn't know what she hoped for. For Kevin

to say he was moving to the other side of the world? For Kevin to say he realized what an idiot he'd been and he wanted her back?

No! She shivered. She didn't want to go back to the life they'd had.

But if he'd changed?

"God, I'm so confused. If you are really there, please, please take the confusion away."

Trista stood outside the sparkling white-and-redbrick eighteenth-century structure with the beautiful tall spire and bell tower. The Chestnut Grove Community Church was a landmark and every effort had been made to preserve the integrity of the building.

With snow blanketing the grounds and the sky overhead a powder blue, the church looked like a Currier and Ives Christmas card. A foreign sense of nostalgia gripped her. How could she miss something she'd never experienced?

She hesitated at the dark, wooden double doors with their antique handles and turn-of-the-century sconces on either side above the sidelight windows. But Scott was waiting and Kevin would arrive shortly, so she opened the door on the right and stepped through the opening. She told herself to be strong, to stay cool.

The inside of the church was as quaint and charming as the outside with dark wood and red carpet runners. The scent of vanilla teased her nose. As she passed a candelabra she discovered the soothing scent. She thought she'd feel like a trespasser but strangely she didn't.

She found her way to the church office. The receptionist buzzed Scott and a moment later he came striding down the hall, looking handsome in a dark suit and red tie. His blond hair was swept back and his strong jaw smooth.

Trista's heart did a little hiccup of welcome. "I know I'm a bit early, but I wanted to arrive first."

"No problem," he said easily and led her past an office with his name on the door. He escorted her to a small conference room that had a round table with three chairs, a box of Kleenex and a water dispenser in the corner.

Pictures of the Virginia Mountains graced walls and windows that looked out onto the historic graveyard in the back of the church brightened the austere space.

Trista took the seat closest to the window. "I've always thought it a bit creepy to have a graveyard so close to a church."

"Many of Chestnut Grove's prominent citizens are buried in that cemetery."

"Oh, so there might be a wealth of buried secrets here?" she teased.

"You don't know how close you are to the truth," Scott said. "Barnaby Harcourt kept a lot of people's secrets in this town."

"I know. Ross is determined to uncover them all and it scares me. I don't want anything to happen to him."

"He's an ex-cop right?"

She nodded and a knot in the pit of her stomach formed. "Those were scary years. But being a private investigator seems to have its danger, too."

"I'm sure he'll be careful."

Trista looked at her watch. Kevin was twenty minutes late. Typical. Irritation bound the knot in her gut tighter. Whenever he was supposed to do something important with her, he had always been late.

"Do you think you should call him?"

She shook her head. "No. He's never been punctual. That was one of the things that really irritated me. He never respects other people's time. He'll come blowing in here as if nothing was wrong and wonder why I'm mad."

There was empathy in his eyes. "Have you two tried counseling before?"

"No. I suggested it and would have gladly gone,

but Kevin always scoffed at it. That's why I was so surprised when he agreed to meet here with you."

"Maybe he's changed. People tend to realize what they've lost once it's gone."

She turned away from his earnestness to stare out the window. "Maybe."

She didn't want Scott to see how upsetting and confusing she found that thought to be. "For Aidan's sake I hope you're right." Though she couldn't see herself getting back together with Kevin, it would be nice if Kevin wanted to be a part of Aidan's life.

"When was the last time Kevin saw Aidan?"

"The day he walked out on us, six months ago." The hurt and anger of that day still throbbed in her chest.

Scott frowned. "He hasn't come to see his son?"

Her mouth twisted with disgust. "He thought parenthood would cramp his style. He wasn't happy when I got pregnant." He'd been livid, in fact. Ranting and raving, demanding to know how she could do this to him, as if she'd poisoned him or something.

"What about his family?"

She shrugged. "His mother came to see Aidan when we were in the hospital. Mr. and Mrs.

Hughes aren't the affectionate type. Since that one visit, I haven't heard from them at all." And she probably wouldn't. They'd never thought her good enough to be a Hughes.

"Have you made the effort?"

Her hackles rose. "Why should I?"

The gentle expression on Scott's face melted her anger. "They may be waiting for you to contact them. A bridge can't be formed if neither side is willing. Sometimes being the bridge builder is what's required."

"Bridge builder." She tried to think that through. Were the Hughes waiting for her to reach out to them? "I don't know if I can. My marriage to their son failed. Why would they want to hear from me?"

"You have their grandson. I'll bet you'd be surprised."

"I'll think about it." It would be good for Aidan to have grandparents. Maybe they'd be better grandparents than parents. She wouldn't get a chance to find out if her own mother would be a better grandparent. She glanced at her watch again. Kevin was an hour late. Annoyance crept up her neck, she could feel her blood pressure rising. "He's not going to show. I should've known."

"Can you call him?"

She blew out a frustrated breath and dug out her cell phone. She punched in Kevin's cell number. His voice mail picked up. She left a quick, terse message, then hung up.

As she hung up, Scott said, his voice soft, "I'm sorry for your disappointment."

She gave him a startled glance. "I'm not. I mean, I'm annoyed as all get out and kicking myself for thinking he'd do as he said. But I'm not disappointed."

"You're not?"

"No." She didn't want to explain that any love she'd had for Kevin had died long ago. She'd only agreed to meet with Kevin for Aidan's sake. She rose. "I'm sorry I wasted your time."

Scott stood and placed a hand on her arm. "I could never think of spending time with you a waste."

The weight of his hand and the meaning of his words wrapped around her like a warm breeze. Why couldn't she have chosen someone like Scott?

He was everything she'd longed for. Stable, honorable, secure. A man who wouldn't be unfaithful, a man who would cherish his wife and son.

But she wasn't looking for a relationship. She

had to get her life under control and make a secure life for Aidan.

She stepped back. "I should go."

"It's lunchtime. How about I buy you a hot dog?"

Swallowing down the urge to say yes, she shook her head. "I should get back to the office."

Scott nodded and led her back to the main hall.

"We can reschedule with Kevin," he said.

"That won't be necessary." Seeing the doubt in Scott's eyes, she confessed, "I asked God to take away my confusion over Kevin. I think being stood up again by him has made it clear to me that he won't change. Kevin's priority will always be Kevin."

"You should give him the benefit of the doubt. He could be stuck in traffic, his cell could have died or be in a blank spot. He could have had an accident."

"You're sweet," she commented, touched by his concern and his eagerness to look for the best in a person. "I've been down this road before. I used to twist myself in knots worrying that something had happened to him every time he was late or didn't show. And it wasn't that he lost track of time like an absentminded person, he just didn't care. His word meant nothing. He hasn't changed."

"Don't make a judgment until you've heard him out," Scott advised.

Trista didn't want to belabor the point, so she nodded. "I'll do my best. Again, thank you for your time."

"I hope you'll come back. I really look forward to getting to know you better."

The longing in his eyes brought her breath to a halt and a corresponding longing flooded through her. The attraction she'd been fighting sparked and charged the air between them. He took a half step forward and then hesitated, as if suddenly realizing he'd moved. The cords in his neck tensed as he swallowed.

"I should get back to work," he said abruptly and walked away.

Bemused by his sudden departure, she stared after him. He'd felt the attraction, too. But he'd turned away from it, from her. She should be glad. She didn't want to ruin the budding friendship they were building with something that could never be. No matter how much she might secretly wish otherwise. A friendship was one thing but a romance was not something she was looking for.

Taking a deep cleansing breath, she headed toward the foyer. The double doors leading to the sanctuary had been closed when she'd first arrived and now stood open as if welcoming her inside.

She stepped to the threshold, her gaze taking in the simple elegance of the beautifully aged wooden pews, the stunning Tiffany stained glass lining the tops of the arched windows and the wooden pulpit at the front of the sanctuary. Candelabras flanked the sides of the altar, along with huge bouquets of flowers.

Compelled for reasons she didn't understand, she crossed the threshold and walked slowly down the aisle. The peaceful quiet of the sanctuary soothed her soul. She paused at the foot of the altar, confused about what to do. Why had she come in here?

She'd asked a question of *Called2serve*. That question came back to her now, as did the answer.

How do I ask Him?

There's nothing complicated about it, even though we'd like to think there is. Open your heart and mind to Him. Ask Him silently or aloud to show you His love, to come into your life.

Scott had said, *Give Him the past and trust Him with your future.*

Could she do those things? Her brother put so

much importance on his faith. He'd found a peace she longed for. Was the same really available to her? After the nightmare of her childhood and the awful ways she'd tried to mask the pain, could God accept her and love her?

Her heart thumped in her chest. As scared as she was to be rejected, she had to ask. She glanced around, verifying she was alone. Slowly she bowed her head and whispered, "Lord, I don't know if you're listening, but I want you in my life. I want what I see in Ross and Kelly. And Scott."

An image of her mother as she remembered her from childhood rose, along with familiar anger followed closely by the pity she now felt at the deteriorated state her mother was currently in. "How do I forgive her? How do I let go of the past?"

The sound of the outer doors opening distracted her. Her heart jumped with dread as she turned, expecting to see Kevin finally arriving. Relief weakened her knees. It wasn't Kevin walking into the sanctuary, but an older woman with red hair and kind eyes.

"I'm sorry. I didn't mean to disturb you," the woman said.

Trista gave her a small embarrassed smile. "That's okay. I was just leaving."

As she left the church behind, she resigned herself to not receiving an answer to her questions.

Scott stepped out of the shadows of the foyer and watched Trista peel out of the parking lot as if she'd stolen something. He hurt for her, for the pain she tried so hard to deny, but was visible in her eyes.

She may have said she was over her ex-husband, but the pain he'd caused her hadn't left.

Scott tried to be charitable in his thoughts about Kevin Hughes, but he was struggling. How could the man have walked away from Trista and Aidan? How could he play such cruel games with her now?

Reminding himself he'd only heard one side of the story and an incomplete account at that, he turned away from the sight of Trista's fleeing car and found himself facing Naomi.

"She's hurting," she stated.

It always amazed him how easily she read people. "Yes, she is. And I'm not sure I can help her."

Naomi gave him a sage nod. "You can. Trust yourself and trust God."

That was advice he'd given out before, but

being on the receiving end felt odd and disquieting. Maybe because of the subject of his doubts? He didn't know how to help Trista while at the same time not letting himself fall for her. There had been a moment earlier when he'd wanted so badly to take her in his arms and soothe the wounds that she so clearly carried.

But giving in to the attraction he felt wouldn't help either of them. She needed his friendship and guidance. And he wasn't looking for a relationship.

No. He had to stay focused on what the Lord would have him do. He had to help her process her pain and lead her to a better understanding of God's love.

And he had to keep his own emotions under wrap.

Lynda stared at the picture blazoned across the society section of the *Chestnut Grove Gazette* of her husband and a buxom brunette, their heads close together like lovers. Her stomach roiled with anger and hurt as she read the accompanying article written by a reporter named Lori Sumner.

When asked about the relationship with the woman pictured above, Douglas Matthews laughed. "Just one of my adoring fans." He once again waved away rumors of a shaky marriage and stated, "My wife and son are the most important things to me."

Things! That's how he saw them. His possessions.

And the woman? Just a fan? Hardly.

She was the same woman Lynda had seen Douglas with once before when he'd thought she and Logan were still out of town. They'd come home early because Logan hadn't felt well. As they'd turned down their street, Douglas and this woman had been coming out of her house.

Correction. Douglas's house.

Lynda slapped the paper onto the kitchen table, startling Logan from his cereal. She winced. "Sorry, dear. Hurry up now or you'll be late for school."

She grabbed the paper so her son wouldn't see the picture, though she was sure he'd hear about it at school. Like always. It pained her to have to send him out into the cruel world where his father's actions were a source of fodder for gossip. She would try to prepare him in the car on the way to school.

She took the paper and moved to throw it in the garbage bin.

"What are you doing?"

Douglas's growled question stopped her cold. Slowly, she turned, her fingers squeezing tight around the paper, crumpling it.

Douglas stood in the doorway of the kitchen, his hands on his hips. The black slacks and bright blue dress shirt made especially for his frame were expensive and trendy, but did little to hide the slight roll of excess fat around his middle. Satisfaction unfurled in her belly. His indulgent lifestyle was starting to show. Petty, she knew but she'd take any small measure of satisfaction.

She shifted her gaze to his face. The hard line of his jaw and the coldness of his blue eyes sent ripples of apprehension over her skin. She fought the sensation, trying hard not to let her fear or her hatred show. She'd made that mistake once and had paid dearly for it.

"Logan, run along now and put your shoes on," she said, her voice sounding too high and strained.

Logan slid from his chair, ducked his head and skirted around his father, who ignored him, before racing up the stairs.

"I asked you a question," Douglas stated and stepped toward her.

She backed up against the counter, desperately wishing it wasn't the housekeeper's day off. Then at least she'd have a buffer, because Douglas would never cause a commotion in front of anyone for fear of a witness.

His precious TV talk show was too important to him for him to take chances that someone could testify that he abused his wife.

"I was just getting Logan his breakfast," she said.

He strode forward and grabbed her wrist. "You were going to throw the paper out before I even had a chance to read it."

She didn't respond as he took the paper and moved to sit at the table. He spread out the wrinkles and stared at his picture. He snorted. "Dumb, dumb, dumb."

She didn't know if he meant himself or the reporter's article.

She thought of Trista and tried to imagine what she would do. Who was she kidding? Trista was a strong woman, Lynda was just Lynda.

"Did you think you could hide this picture from me?" He slanted her a hard glance. "You know I collect all my press." He rose.

Lynda gripped the edge of the counter and ducked her head. "I didn't want Logan to see it."

"You coddle him too much. He needs to grow

up. The world is what it is. Fame and fortune come at a price."

"I pay it," she muttered, the words escaping before she could stop them.

He grabbed her arm in a painful grip. "What did you say?"

She grimaced with alarm. "Nothing. I need to take Logan to school."

With a powerful jerk he dragged her toward the den.

Dread and hate slithered over her as she tried to stop the forward momentum but the soles of her slick flats slid across the polished hardwood. "Logan will be late."

He flung open the den door and pushed her inside. "Write him a note."

As he slammed the door shut behind him, Lynda braced herself for what was to come and silently raged inside her head.

Chapter Seven

Ross closed the file he'd just finished cross-referencing with the documents the agency had on file. So far no other falsified records had been discovered from this new batch. He wasn't sure why Barnaby Harcourt had hidden these ones away.

Leaning back in his chair, Ross picked up his coffee mug and savored the strong brew. Letting his mind wander from the business at hand, he thought about his mother and Trista and the day at the nursing home.

He should have prepared Trista before taking her there, but he'd wanted her to see for herself how badly their mother was doing. He hadn't wanted her to harden her heart prior to going there any more than she had already.

She still resented the way their childhood had

gone and harbored anger at their parents. Even though he'd made his peace with his parents and the past, he didn't blame her. Mom and Dad had been selfish, wounded people who needed help.

And Ross was determined not to make the same mistakes with his own child. And he prayed that Trista would come to know some peace.

Thankfully, Kevin wasn't in the picture. Ross's hand tightened around the mug. He'd known Kevin wasn't the right man for his sister and he'd told Trista as much. In this instance, Ross hated having been right.

With a sigh, he sat forward and picked up another file. The tab read Wendy Kates.

Inside he found a birth certificate for a baby girl with an unnamed father and the pediatrician's records. The last paper in the folder was a ledger showing large payments being paid on the fifth of every month. Ross's heart sped up.

Someone was paying off Harcourt to keep quiet about this child and her mother. He flipped back through the pages, reading more carefully. He set his jaw with anger when he came across a small, handwritten notation of a sum of money and the initials LM in the corner of the hospital records.

LM. Who could that be?

Ross typed the name Wendy Kates into the

computer. No record of her was found. This file
didn't have a duplicate in the system, which could
only mean that whoever was paying off Barnaby
was someone with a lot of money and influence.

Ross grabbed the file and his coat. He'd check
the records at the hospital. They had to have a file
on Wendy Kates. If he could track down the
mother, then he could find out what the money had
been for and who LM was.

He wouldn't let this blemish on the reputation
of Tiny Blessings Adoption agency be a stain
much longer.

Lynda hurried Logan to the play structure in the
middle of Winchester Park. Several moms sat
bundled up on the park benches as their kids
played in the snow and on the equipment. After
school, Logan had pleaded to be able to join the
boys from school and Lynda decided playtime
would be a good cover if asked why they'd been
in the park.

There was a pay phone not far from the play-
ground. Since she couldn't risk using the home
phone, she could use the pay phone and keep an
eye on Logan at the same time.

Logan started playing with another boy.

Lynda hurried to the pay phone. Taking her

hands out of her woolen gloves, she reached in her pocket for Trista Van Zandt's card. Lynda picked up the receiver and paused as she noticed Detective Fletcher get out of his patrol car, put on a coat and meet a brunette woman near the baseball field.

Lynda turned away, shielding her face, though she doubted Detective Fletcher would be able to recognize her beneath the stocking cap, big glasses and zipped-up parka. Quickly, before she lost her nerve, she dialed the number on the card. When the receptionist answered Lynda asked for Ms. Van Zandt.

Trista answered a moment later. "This is Trista."

Lynda's voice stuck in her throat as it had the last time she'd tried to call her. Then she'd tried Trista's home phone but she'd lost the nerve to talk.

"Hello? Is anyone there?"

Kicking herself in gear, Lynda nodded. "Yes."

"Lynda? Is that you?"

Suddenly the words poured out.

"Yes. I don't know what else to do. I have to find a way to protect myself and Logan. I didn't know who else to call. I certainly can't call the police. The scandal would enrage Douglas and who knows what he'd do then," Lynda said in a flurry of words.

"Lynda, calm down. You made the right move in calling me. Where are you?"

"I…can we meet?"

"Of course. Why don't you come to my office?"

Panicked, Lynda hunched her shoulders. She could never be seen at a lawyer's office. "Oh, no. That wouldn't be wise." She frantically thought of a place that would be private enough to talk but not unusual for her and Logan to be at. "Can we meet at the library in the children's section on Saturday?"

"Saturday at the library. What time?"

Lynda gave a fugitive glance around and nearly dropped the phone when she noticed the crew van for Douglas's show setting up on the hill. He usually did the show in the studio. Why today was he doing it outside? "Ten," she said quickly and hung up.

She rushed over to Logan and promised him ice cream to get him to leave. She didn't want to be in the park with Douglas anywhere around.

The buzz of a cell phone interrupted the man midsentence. He smiled an apology before moving off to the side to answer. His polished shoes sank into the snow but his long woolen coat kept the chill at bay.

A young woman's voice said, "Sir, you said to call if anyone asked about the files you mentioned."

The man's gut twisted. "Yes."

"Well, a Mr. Van Zandt came in to the records department here at the hospital. I overheard him ask for the Wendy Kates records."

Rage choked the man. He took deep breaths to calm himself. "I'll make sure you're well paid for this information."

"Thank you, sir."

The man put the phone away and his hands shook slightly, betraying his inner chaos.

His carefully made plan wasn't working!

The man slammed one fist into the palm of his other hand. The Van Zandts weren't backing off their investigation into Harcourt's dirty dealings. If they didn't soon, everything he had worked so hard to achieve would be destroyed. One indiscretion wasn't going to bring him down.

Something had to be done.

Standing in the center of Winchester Park, right in the heart of downtown Chestnut Grove, he had a clear view of the bustling town square. People blithely went about their day, oblivious to his growing agitation.

An elderly couple, bundled in warm coats to

ward off the chill of the cold fall day, ambled along the path that followed the man-made pond. A teenager threw a Frisbee for a black lab to catch. Children frolicked on the play structure.

A few feet away from the man, a woman pushed a stroller with a swaddled infant barely visible inside on a paved path through the park. She slanted him an interested smile, which he acknowledged with a nod. Watching the tall, leggy redhead weave her way to the other side of the park, an idea formed in his mind.

His lip curled up. Yes, he knew the perfect way to get his point across to the Van Zandts. This time he'd get personal. Very personal.

"Sir, is everything all right?" A young doe-eyed woman touched his arm.

Clearing his expression, the man turned to give the girl a wolfish grin and she smiled back. Ah, but he loved to see that adoring expression on females. A response that allowed him free rein. He linked her arm through his and stroked her hand. "Everything will be just fine."

Lynda guided Logan toward the children's section of the library. She kept her gaze downcast and averted from what Douglas told her were the prying eyes of the public. She wore a hat pulled low over her bruised ear where Douglas had slapped her.

He was becoming increasingly careless. First the black eye and now her ear. Before he would always take out his frustration with her on parts of her body that didn't show.

She hunched her stiff and sore shoulders where she'd taken most of his hits the other day. Thankfully, he'd left her alone since then.

She was sure Logan's teacher sensed something was wrong when they'd arrived at class an hour late with her moving slow and trying not to let the pain show. But no one ever said anything. No one, that is, except Trista Van Zandt.

Everyone was too blinded by the fact that Douglas Matthews, one of the town's own sons, had made it to the big time with his own talk show. No one wanted to see what he was really like—a spoiled, grasping, violent man with deep insecurities stemming from overindulgent parents who gave in to his every whim.

Logan squeezed her hand and pointed to the bank of computers. Lynda smiled and got him settled at the computer with a game. Douglas refused to allow them a computer at home. It would taint their minds, he'd said.

Just another way for him to control them.

Lynda moved to a table near the window that faced the back alley but still afforded her a view of Logan. She wasn't sure calling Trista had been a good idea. But it would be good to have someone to talk to.

She watched her son smile as he played the computer game. Love welled in her heart and her eyes burned. She wiped at her tears as she saw Trista approaching.

Trista slid into the chair opposite her. "Are you okay?"

Lynda gave her a wan smile. Of course she wasn't okay. "Thank you for coming."

Trista reached out and pushed Lynda's hair aside and revealed her bruised ear. "Don't tell me another baseball accident."

Shame for the lie she'd told brought fresh tears to the surface. She shook her head and covered her ear with her hand.

"It's your husband, isn't it?"

Lynda lifted her gaze. "He just gets so angry with me. I try to be a good wife, but sometimes I speak out of turn."

Trista held up a hand. "Whoa. Please don't make excuses for him. He has no right to hurt you."

Lynda shrank back. "He wasn't always like this.

In the beginning he was real sweet and giving. But as his career has grown, so has his anger toward me. I don't know what I did."

"You are not to blame." Trista's blue eyes darkened with concern. "He needs help."

"Oh, he would never go to a counselor. That would be bad for his image."

"Worse than being a wife batterer?"

Lynda glanced around. "Shh. Someone might hear. He'd get so angry if he knew I was talking to you about this."

Trista nodded and leaned forward. "Let me help you."

"Is there a legal way to get him to stop without making the situation public?"

"Is his public image worth more than your life? Logan's life?"

Desperation and shame clogged her throat. "There has to be a way to protect us without making things worse."

Taking her hand, Trista said, "Listen to me. You have to file a complaint. Is there someone you and Logan can stay with?"

Anxiety twisted around her insides, making her ache. "Oh, I couldn't leave him. I made a commitment before God."

Trista stared at her in disbelief. "What about the

commitment Douglas made before God? He's violated that."

"I'm not sure Douglas knows God. Besides, that's his sin, not mine. I can't sin by leaving him. I won't put my soul in jeopardy."

"I doubt God would consider it a sin if you left your abusive husband," Trista whispered harshly.

Lynda's shoulders sagged even more. "I went to the wife of the pastor that married us and she said I needed to be a better wife and to love him more. She suggested new cookbooks. Douglas doesn't like my cooking."

Trista wanted to come out of her skin with anger. How could a woman, a pastor's wife at that, tell another woman such garbage? "Obviously, this woman was delusional. You have to listen to me, no one has the right to hurt you, especially the man who's supposed to love you. You are not to blame and you aren't alone in this. You have to think of Logan. Men who are violent usually don't change. Eventually, he'll turn his anger onto your son."

Pure horror swept through Lynda. She shook her head. "He wouldn't do that."

"Are you willing to risk your son's life?" Trista asked, in a harsh tone.

Lynda swallowed, the fear hitting her stomach

and making it roll. "I couldn't leave him. I wouldn't know where to go. I have no way to support Logan and myself. I can't get a divorce. I just can't. Besides, he'd find me anyway and just bring us back."

The tears streaming down Lynda's face made Trista's heart spasm with compassion. "I've been where you are. My ex-husband was very controlling and manipulative. He alienated me from my family and friends. He made my world about him. But then I became pregnant and realized that I had a life outside of myself to protect. I didn't want to admit my marriage had failed. But it had. And I'm okay."

"You think God has forgiven you?"

Trista bit her lip. She wasn't sure how to answer because she'd never thought of it. "I've only recently allowed God into my life."

Lynda nodded. "Then you're safe. But I wouldn't be."

"What do you think will happen?"

"He'll punish me."

"Like how Douglas punishes you?"

For a moment Lynda looked speechless. "I don't know. I'm just so scared."

"Then let me help you," Trista pleaded, fear for Lynda knotting in her chest.

"I don't think you can." Lynda stood. "I'm sorry."

Trista watched helplessly as Lynda collected her son and they left the library. Frustration beat a steady rhythm behind Trista's eyes. She'd been so ineffective, so ill equipped to convince Lynda that God wouldn't punish her for protecting herself and her son. How could Lynda stay with Douglas?

Trista rubbed at her temples. What could she do to help Lynda?

An idea floated in her mind. Resolutely, she pulled out her cell phone and called Chestnut Grove Community Church. She asked to be put through to Scott.

"This is Scott."

Just hearing his voice calmed her agitation. She'd made the right decision. "Scott, it's Trista. I need your help."

She told him the situation and asked if he'd see Lynda.

"Of course I will. I was hoping that wasn't the case. You called it right at the bookstore that day. I think we need to proceed cautiously. We wouldn't want to make things worse for her. The Matthewses attend the 10:00 a.m. service on Sunday mornings. Why don't you come and then we can talk with Lynda in a nonthreatening manner, see if she'll agree to meet privately."

Relief to be able to share the burden with him coursed through her. "That would be great. Thank you." Trista hung up.

Resting her elbows on the table, she supported her head with her hands. She was going to church in the morning. She wasn't sure how she felt about that.

Like it or not, for Lynda's sake, she had to go.

Sunday morning arrived with a bitter wind and snow flurries. Trista bundled up Aidan and drove them to the church. She parked near Kelly's car and carried Aidan toward the entrance. Small clusters of people gathered to talk, while others either hurried inside for the second service of the day or rushed to their cars after the early service.

Scott stood near the double doors, his long trench coat tied at his waist and his ears turning red from the weather. Her heart lifted with a smile as he spotted them and came forward.

"Good morning, you two," he said, his gaze warm.

"Good morning," she responded, feeling suddenly shy at how obvious it was that he'd been waiting for them.

"I'm glad you came," he stated as they walked.

"You thought I wouldn't?"

His eyes twinkled. "I was praying you wouldn't chicken out."

"Hey!" she protested with a chuckle, though the truth was she had almost backed out. If it weren't for the fact that she needed to talk with Lynda again, she probably wouldn't have come. Her faith was too new for her to really embrace sitting in church.

With trepidation, she hesitated outside the big doors leading to the sanctuary.

"It's going to be okay," Scott said softly.

Taking comfort in his presence, she nodded. "Have the Matthewses arrived?"

"They're seated already." He led her inside. "Let's take Aidan to the nursery room."

Trista followed Scott down a hallway, passing kids and parents along the way. They stopped at a gated door to a room filled with toys and soothing music. There were several women of various ages in the nursery taking care of the infants, including her sister-in-law, Kelly.

"Kelly, what are you doing in here?" Trista asked.

Kelly sat in a rocker holding a little girl dressed all in pink. "I help out every other Sunday. I'm so glad to see you and my nephew." She rose and handed the little girl to another woman before ambling over to take Aidan.

"Go enjoy the service. We'll be fine." Kelly shooed Trista and Scott away.

Scott touched her elbow. Just a slight pressure but it felt warm and comforting. He led her back toward the sanctuary and paused at the coatrack to help her with her parka.

"Shouldn't you be up onstage or something?" she asked.

"I'm running the youth group next door. I'll get you seated and then head over there."

He wouldn't be in the service? She felt very alone as he found her a seat in a pew near the front, not far from where the Matthews family sat. Lynda briefly made eye contact before shifting her gaze straight ahead. Trista wondered why Logan sat with his parents. Shouldn't he be in a class for his age group?

Trista glanced around noting familiar faces. Some she knew by name, others just in passing. Detective Fletcher and his wife sat off to her right. Kelly's assistant, Eric, sat behind them with his girlfriend Samantha Harcourt. Off to her left sat the Noble clan. She also saw the woman she'd seen in the sanctuary the last time she'd been here.

A small group of people rose and went to the musical instruments on the stage. Within moments music filled the church. Trista listened, letting the words and the melodies run through her, stirring her spirit and refreshing her soul.

When the music ended, Reverend Fraser walked out to the podium. His brown eyes, behind wire-rimmed glasses, touched briefly on Trista before he began speaking. His voice was pleasant to listen to. He had a very natural and unassuming way about him. He spoke about giving thanks for everything which was an appropriate message considering Thanksgiving was just a little over a week away.

Trista enjoyed the commentaries and the little jokes the Reverend interspersed into his sermon. When he was done and the music once again filled the church, Trista realized she hadn't once felt lost or confused. And she *was* thankful for her life, her son. No matter what else had happened or would happen, she would always give thanks for her baby.

As the service let out and people began to fill the aisles, Trista maneuvered so she was behind Lynda as they filed out of the sanctuary.

Trista leaned in close to whisper, "Meet me in the ladies' room."

Lynda gave a barely perceivable nod.

A few minutes later Trista stood in the ante-chamber of the women's lounge. Plush small sofas and armchairs sat across from a mirrored wall with hand lotion dispensers and tissue boxes on the counter that ran along the wall underneath the mirror.

Lynda came in like a scared rabbit, held her finger to her lips before checking to see that there was no one else in the restroom. She hurried over to Trista and took her hand. "I'm so glad to see you. I didn't know you attended our church."

"This is my first time here."

Lynda smiled. "Welcome, then."

"Would you be willing to meet with Pastor Scott?"

Lynda's eyes grew big. "I don't know. I wouldn't want him to think badly of me or Douglas."

Kind of hard not to think badly of Douglas, Trista thought but refrained from saying aloud. "He's not going to judge you. He only wants to help."

"Well, I guess it couldn't hurt," Lynda stated. "Would you be there?"

"If you'd like me to."

"I would." Lynda edged toward the door. "Thursday, noon, at the library?"

"I'm sure that would be fine."

"Okay, then," Lynda murmured before slipping out the door.

Trista sighed with relief. Giving Lynda a few moments head start, Trista went in search of her son. She found Aidan and Kelly still in the nursery.

"How did he do?" Trista asked.

Kelly smiled as she wiped down a toy with a cleaning rag. "He did great. He's so much fun." Kelly put the toy away and picked up another. "How about you? Did you enjoy the service?"

Trista nodded. More than she'd expected. "Very much." She picked up Aidan and snuggled him close.

"What are your plans today?" Kelly asked.

"I brought home some work to do while Aidan takes his nap. Then I thought I'd take him to the park if the weather holds."

"That sounds fun," Scott said as he came into the room. "Would you care for some company?"

Trista ignored the amused glint in Kelly's gaze as she turned to greet Scott. His easy smile and gentle eyes made her heart sputter. She'd enjoyed spending time with him the other day when Kevin had blown off their appointment. Besides, she decided, it'd be nice to have the company. "That would be great. He'll be up about three."

"Perfect." Scott grinned. "I'll come by your place."

"Okay."

He waved and left.

"Another nondate?"

Trista slanted a glance to her sister-in-law. "Honestly? I don't know."

Chapter Eight

A knock at the front door jolted Trista's concentration from the legal brief in front of her. She glanced at the oak wall clock. Scott was early. Bubbles of anticipation rose heating her cheeks.

She unfolded herself from the couch, checked her hair in the mirror on the wall and went to the door. She peered through the peephole expecting to see Scott.

Instead, her ex-husband, Kevin, stood there. The bubbles burst with stinging pops.

His long, London Fog coat showed no signs of the weather outside and his black hair was perfectly in place. Tall and lean, Kevin always dressed impeccably, a trait he'd learned from his wealthy parents. Appearances were everything to the Hughes family.

She leaned forward against the hard wood of the

door. Annoyance tightened her chest. If she ignored him, would he go away? He knocked again and she jumped back.

Afraid that his banging would wake Aidan, she yanked the door open.

"Hi, babe," Kevin said, his charming, boyish grin in place.

Once she'd loved that smile, now, thank goodness, it did nothing for her. "Kevin, what are you doing here?"

"Are you going to invite me in?"

Rancor sharpened her voice. "No."

His brown eyes darkened. "I just want to talk." He held out his hand palm up. "Honest."

She crossed her arms over her chest. "About what?"

"Us."

Her stomach clenched tight as if she'd just received a kick in the gut. "There is no *us*. You walked out." She gritted her teeth and added, "Left me for another woman."

"Can I at least explain?"

His saccharine-sweet tone sent warning bells banging in her head like the sound of a gavel hitting the judge's bench. He'd used that tone every time he wanted his way. "I don't need to hear your excuses."

A door opened down the hall. "I'd rather not

have your neighbors know our business," he said and moved closer.

With a sigh of resigned frustration because she, too, didn't want to air her dirty laundry, she widened the door and stepped back. Kevin strode in, his Italian loafers making no noise on the carpet. His expression as he glanced around was one of distaste. "Interesting place."

Hanging on to her rising temper, Trista said, "So why did you come here, Kevin?"

He faced her, his dark eyes warm and his smile coaxing. "I miss you. I miss us."

Bile rose in her throat. "Until the next woman catches your fancy?" Trista shook her head. "We've been down that road."

"I promise this time will be different. I'm different," he assured her as he stepped closer.

The familiar scent of his aftershave burned her nose. "Where were you on Tuesday?"

His dark eyebrows dipped together. "Tuesday?"

She waved away his question with an impatient gesture. There was no point in calling him on standing up her and Scott. "Forget it."

"Don't you miss us? Miss the fun we had?" He swept his arm wide. "You can't enjoy living like this. If you come back to me, I'll buy a big house with a garden. I know you love gardens."

"I don't—" Knowing he wouldn't understand that her decision wasn't about material things, she said, "Did you really come here to try to get back with me?"

"Yes. You're my wife."

She clenched her fist. "No. I'm your ex-wife. You divorced me, remember?"

"I remember," he replied.

"You haven't once asked about Aidan," she stated.

For a moment his expression went blank and then realization hit. "My son. Where is he?"

"Sleeping." She glanced at the clock. Aidan would wake up soon and Scott would arrive shortly after. She could wake Aidan if Kevin showed some interest but the man hadn't even thought about his child, so why should she bother?

"Kevin, you need to go now."

"Let me take you out. Like old times," he said.

Incredible. Why hadn't she realized how thick in the head he was sooner? "No. Aidan will be awake soon."

He studied her with a speculative gleam. "He's very important to you?"

Duh? "Yes. He's everything to me. And he should be to you. You're his father."

"That's true," he murmured.

She didn't like the way his gaze sharpened. He may be thick in some ways but he was also smart. "Look, Kevin. I don't know what you hoped to accomplish today, but Aidan and I have plans. So I'd like it if you left now."

"I'll go with you," he said.

Exasperation beat at her temple. "That wouldn't—"

A knock interrupted her. Oh, no! Scott. Could this day get any worse?

Bracing herself, she opened the door. Scott was a welcome and calming sight. His blond hair was wind tossed and his checks ruddy from the cold. He wore a big parka, jeans and snow boots.

"Hi, come in," she said.

He grinned. "Hope you're ready to play…" He stopped as he saw Kevin, who was sporting a look of outrage.

"Scott, this is my *ex*-husband, Kevin Hughes. Kevin, Scott…Pastor Scott Crosby."

Stiffly, Scott extended his hand. "Hello."

Kevin's thunderous expression shifted and became probing. He shook Scott's hand. "A pastor? Well, that's good timing."

Trista frowned as unease tickled the hair at her nape. "Kevin was just leaving."

Kevin shook his head and gave her an indulgent

smile. "No, I was trying to convince you to give our marriage another chance." He turned to Scott. "So, Pastor, maybe you can convince Trista not to hold the past against me. You do believe in the sanctity of marriage, don't you?"

Trista wanted to scream. How dare Kevin talk about the sanctity of marriage when he'd done everything he could to destroy their marriage.

"Of course, I do," Scott replied woodenly.

She heard a cry from the bedroom. Aidan waking from his nap. Trista was torn between getting Aidan up and staying to make sure Kevin left.

Kevin stepped close and kissed her cheek. She recoiled at his touch. She didn't want his kisses or his presence in her life.

"I'll be in touch," he stated and left.

Trista stared at the closed door. "Unbelievable." She turned her gaze to Scott. The strange, remote expression on his face confused her. "I'm sorry about that."

"He's right, you know. You should give your marriage another chance. For Aidan's sake."

"You don't know what you're saying."

He sighed. "I have to advocate for the union that you both committed to when you married."

Astounded by his statement she raised her

eyebrows. "I gave Kevin plenty of chances before Aidan was born. I naively thought a child would make a difference. He didn't. I'm not going through all that again."

Aidan cried out again, obviously wanting to be rescued from his crib.

"Can we discuss this another time?" she asked as she headed toward the hall.

"I better go."

She stopped in her tracks. "What? Why?"

His eyes reflected a troubled light. "I'm a pastor, Trista. I can't…I mean, I have to do what's right in the sight of God."

"And you leaving is the right thing to do?"

"Yes. You need to pray about this situation. Let God guide you." He backed toward the door. "I hope I'll see you next Sunday at church." Then he left.

Stunned and confused, Trista dropped her head into her palm. She wasn't sure if she were more angry that Kevin had barged into her life or that Scott had just abandoned her.

Feeling alone and confused, she decided she had no business expecting anything from Scott.

As he stated, he was her pastor, nothing more.

Later that night, Scott sat in his small one-bedroom apartment staring out the living room window. Snow stuck to the edges of the glass and dusted the oak trees outside.

Despite his best intentions, he hadn't done a very good job of controlling his emotions or his attraction to Trista.

When she'd shown up at church, his heart had bounced so hard he was sure it would hit the ceiling. She'd looked so lovely in her navy skirt, high boots and white sweater. Her hair had been bound back in a clip at the base of her graceful neck.

He'd impulsively invited himself to the park with her, telling himself it would be an opportunity to help her, but his motivation was far less altruistic. He simply enjoyed being with her and Aidan.

But she was off-limits. He was a pastor, and as such, needed to be an advocate for marriage. She may not be legally married now, but if there was the slightest possibility that she and Kevin could work things out, Scott had to honor and encourage them.

Regardless of his feelings for Trista.

Even though Scott couldn't be totally objective, he hadn't liked Kevin. The man had been too charming, too smooth. Scott had seen the possessive anger in Kevin's eyes before he realized he could use Scott to his advantage by encouraging Scott to influence Trista and to reinforce the sanctity of marriage.

Lord, this is a strange situation I find myself in and I don't know how to proceed. I really need some clarity.

Scott had ducked out on Trista because retreat was always his first reaction. He understood enough about human psychology to realize he found safety in retreating. But he wouldn't be able to avoid talking to Trista for long. His feelings for her wouldn't allow it. He really cared about her and Aidan.

He would just have to remember to be her pastor and friend. And not let himself become anything else.

"Kelly, these documents require your signature and then need to get to the courthouse this morning before the Cardinellies can adopt baby Joe. They're in my office right now," Pilar said as she swept into Kelly's office and laid the papers on the desk.

Kelly picked up a pen, read the pages and then signed where appropriate. "Have Eric run them downtown."

Pilar shook her head. "He's interviewing a

couple right now. Is Ross around? I was thinking maybe he could run over there."

Kelly shook her head. "He's at the hospital checking out some old records." She heaved herself to her feet. Blood rushed to her brain. She shouldn't have stayed seated for so long. The baby protested the movement with a nice jab of an elbow or knee. Kelly wasn't sure which poky little body part was where. The baby tended to turn and twist a lot.

"I'll take it over," she said, once she regained her equilibrium.

"No, no. I'll call a messenger service."

Shrugging into her wool coat, Kelly smiled. "I'd like some fresh air and I'll see if Trista's free for lunch."

Concern showed in Pilar's beautiful dark, Latin eyes. "Are you sure?"

Picking up her purse and taking out her keys, Kelly nodded. "Yes. I'm not an invalid. Besides, the doctor said it was good for me to stay active." She scooped up the documents and put them in a file folder.

Pilar moved aside to let Kelly pass. "I'll let the Cardenillies know."

On her way out, Kelly let the receptionist know where she was going in case Ross called. As soon as she stepped outside a cold blast of wind hit her. She ducked her head against the biting air and carefully hurried to her car.

Once inside, she cranked up the heat and the CD player. She had a CD of Mozart in because baby experts agreed that classical music stimulated the brain development of a fetus. She didn't know if the theory was true or not, but the music soothed her.

She pulled out of the parking lot and drove at a sedate speed along the busy road leading to downtown Chestnut Grove.

The baby kicked.

"Whoa, little one. Mommy's driving. Let's not distract her," she cooed aloud.

Up ahead the road curved sharply. She pressed her foot on the brake. For a moment the pedal depressed slowly, then with a little jolt the tension disappeared. She pumped her foot on the brake, but nothing happened. Terror slammed into her with the force of an avalanche. She tried to make the turn but she was going too fast.

"Dear Jesus, help," she cried as the back tires slid, sending the car into a sideways slide down into the ditch.

The car came to a jolting stop. The seat belt yanked painfully across Kelly's lower abdomen.

Her hands gripped the steering wheel. Sharp pain stabbed at her belly, cinching her waist and trapping her breath in her chest.

She couldn't breathe. She fought off the wave of darkness descending but it was too strong.

"Oh, God, please…"

"Trista, there's been an accident. Your sister-in-law has been taken to Children's Hospital in Richmond."

Trista stared at her boss for a moment while the words he'd spoken sank in. Harvey Benson's gray eyes were filled with concern beneath his bushy white brows.

Her heart squeezed tight in her chest as panic and fear blurred her vision. She jumped up from her chair and hurried out the door without a word.

She rode the elevator down to the parking garage, the whole time praying that Kelly and the baby would be okay.

She sped to Richmond, thankful for the light traffic. All she could think about was Kelly and the baby.

At the hospital, she parked as close to the entrance as possible and then ran as fast as she could to the emergency doors. Once inside she headed straight to the administration desk.

"Kelly Van Zandt? She was brought in recently."

The kindly looking older woman behind the desk hit the keys on the computer. "She's been taken to the fifth floor for delivery."

"Delivery?" She gasped. The baby wasn't due for another month. Trista raced through the hospital up to the maternity ward where she again stopped at the nurses' desk. "Kelly Van Zandt?"

"She's in delivery. Her husband is in the waiting area," the young blond nurse said.

Trista hurried to the waiting area. Ross sat in one of the fabric-covered chairs, his head in his hands. The room was filled with other familiar people. Pilar, with tears streaking down her checks, clung to her husband, Zach. Eric sat in the corner, his complexion pale. Reverend Fraser and his wife, Naomi, sat beside Ross.

Trista knelt in front of her brother and put her arms around him. Her heart twisted with anguish at seeing her brother so distraught.

He hugged her close, his tears soaking into her blouse. "She slid into a ditch. The baby's coming."

Trista nodded and stroked his hair, much the way he'd done with her when she was young and needed his comfort.

Ross pulled himself together. His face had

seemed to age with his terror. "Someone needs to call Sandra Lange, Kelly's mother."

"I'll do it," Naomi volunteered as she rose and went in search of a phone.

Ross's gaze zeroed in on Zach. "Where's the car?"

"I had it taken in. We'll check to make sure this was just an accident," Zach assured him.

Trista could feel the tension and fear in Ross. "Of course it was an accident. Why would—?" She paused, thinking about the fires, the broken windshield and the threatening notes. "Surely someone wouldn't try to *kill* Kelly and the baby."

Ross stared at her for a moment and she saw that he believed someone had. Shock and paralyzing fear washed over her, mingling with the anguish of knowing they could lose both Kelly and the baby. Her insides twisted with dread of what that would do to her brother.

"Sandra's on her way," Naomi stated as she returned, with Scott just behind her.

Trista gasped softly when she saw him. Compassion, so evident on his face, made fresh tears spring to her eyes. He came straight to her and laid a hand on her shoulder.

She rose and without worrying about the consequences, went into his embrace. His big solid frame wrapped around her, shielding her from the pain of what had happened. For a moment she allowed herself to indulge in the comfort he offered. He was so steady and safe.

A man worth hanging on to.

Only…she pulled away. He wasn't the man for her. He'd made that clear. He was here as a pastor, nothing more.

An aching emptiness replaced his comfort.

She moved to sit on the arm of the chair beside Ross and wrapped her arms around her middle as if somehow doing so would make the emptiness and terror gnawing at her go away.

A tall man in green scrubs approached Ross. His kind eyes surveyed the group. "I'm Doctor Eli Cavanaugh." He and Ross shook hands. "Both mommy and baby are doing well."

Sighs of relief echoed through the waiting room. Ross dropped his head into his hands. "Thank you, God."

The doctor continued, "Kelly's resting. She suffered a few minor bruises and a broken wrist, which we reset, and should heal quickly. The baby's small and his lungs need more incubation time, but overall he's good. He's a fighter."

Ross bolted to his feet. "I have a son?"

Dr. Cavanaugh smiled. "You have a son."

Excited and overjoyed, Trista wrapped her arms around Ross's waist again and hugged him close. She had a nephew. A playmate for Aidan. She couldn't wait to see the newest addition to the family.

"Can I see Kelly?" Ross asked.

"Yes, you may," the doctor replied. "The rest of you will need to wait awhile."

Ross left with Dr. Cavanaugh and Trista breathed a huge sigh of relief. Eric and Pilar hugged each other and then hugged the Frasers. Scott's understanding smile wrapped around Trista like a soothing embrace.

Her heart cried out to go to him, but she fought the impulse and turned away, denying herself anything more from him.

Ross sat at Kelly's bedside watching her sleep. She was the most beautiful, tough and generous woman he'd ever known. If he'd lost her, he didn't know what he would have done.

Their baby boy lay in an enclosed bed in another room where his little body was hooked up to monitors and machines. He was so tiny and helpless. And even though the doctor assured Ross his son was doing well, he'd wept when he'd seen his child.

Kelly stirred, her eyelids fluttered then opened. She gave him a small smile. "Hi."

His heart squeezed. "Hi, Mom."

Her smile grew and her eyes shined. "How is he?"

"Good. The doctor said he'll need to stay in the neonatal ICU for a while but he's strong and beautiful."

"Cameron?"

Ross nodded. "Cameron."

Kelly closed her eyes. "I don't know what happened. One second the brakes were working and then they weren't."

Ross's jaw tightened. He forced his voice to stay neutral. "What matters is that you and Cameron are safe now."

She took his hand. "Yes."

"I'm going to stop my investigations. The risk to you and Cameron is too great."

She stared at him. "You don't think this was an accident?"

"No."

"You can't let whoever did this win! The adoptees deserve to know the truth. And we'll never discover who's behind all of this if you back off."

There was a knock on the door a second

before it opened and Zach stuck his head in. He gave Ross a quick nod to indicate he needed to speak with him before Zach disappeared, shutting the door behind him.

Ross leaned in to kiss Kelly. "I'll be back in a few."

"Hmm. Okay. Be careful," she replied sleepily.

Ross found Zach waiting for him in the hall. "What's up?"

His eyes were hard and his jaw set in a grim line. "The brake line had been cut."

Ross pounded his fist into the wall, startling a passing nurse. "I'm going to find out who's responsible and when I do—"

Zach put his hand on Ross's shoulder. "You need to concentrate on your family. Let me take care of this."

"Like you have with everything else," Ross barked.

Zach drew back. "Hey, buddy. I'm doing my best."

Ross blew out a harsh breath. "I know. I'm sorry. This is just too much."

"We'll catch the person responsible. The forensic team is thoroughly searching the car and where the car was parked. We'll canvass for witnesses, see if anyone remembers someone in the parking lot."

Ross nodded, knowing that was the protocol and if there were any clues the team would find them. He felt so helpless and vulnerable. His family had almost been killed.

"I better get back," Zach stated. "Oh, and be aware there's a news crew in the lobby."

That gave Ross an idea. "I'll walk you out."

In the lobby, Ross went straight for the news crew. The reporter, a guy in his late thirties wearing a dark green suit and yellow tie, eagerly asked Ross for a statement.

"Oh, I have a statement all right," Ross announced. He looked straight into the camera. "Tiny Blessings Adoption agency will never stop searching for the truth and repairing the damage that has been done to so many families. And whoever tried to kill my wife today, I will find you. Then you will pay!"

Chapter Nine

Trista leaned her head against the back of the hospital waiting room chair. Around her the staff of Tiny Blessings, the Frasers and Scott sat chatting quietly. The soft click of heels on the hard surface of the floor drew Trista's attention.

Sandra Lange, Kelly's biological mother, and Sandra's friend Tony Conlon, approached. Kelly had been stolen from Sandra at birth and the two had recently been reunited. Sandra was shorter than her daughter and plump. She'd recently battled breast cancer and was apparently doing well now.

"Please, tell me Kelly is okay," Sandra said to the group. Her worried green eyes searched them all and landed on Trista.

Trista rose and went to her. "Kelly's a little

banged up, but otherwise good. The baby's a boy and the doctor said he'll be fine."

Sandra sagged with relief. "How did this happen?"

Trista shook her head. "We don't know yet. Ross is in with Kelly now. I'm sure you'll be allowed to see her soon."

Sandra headed to the nurses' station. Kelly was lucky to have found her mother and to have developed such a close bond. Trista would always regret that she'd spent so many years angry with her mother and now would never have a chance to bond with her.

When Sandra reached the nurses' station, a tall African-American male nurse seemed to ask a question at which Sandra pointed back toward the group. The nurse then came down the hall.

"Excuse me. Is there a Trista Van Zandt here?"

"I'm Trista."

The man waved her forward. "There's a call for you at the desk."

Trista followed the nurse. Who could be calling her? No one knew she was here except her boss.

She picked up the phone. "Hello, this is Trista Van Zandt."

"Trista, it's Harvey Benson. How's your sister-in-law?"

Her boss. "She's going to be okay."

"Well, that's a relief. I hate to be the bearer of more bad news, but a Mrs. Angelo called. She wants you to call the nursing home right away."

Trista gripped the phone as a sudden jolt of dread and apprehension shot through her. "Thank you. I'll call right now."

After hanging up, she stood there, her heart pounding, her thoughts racing. Had something happened to her mother? Had she passed on? Trista began to shake.

"Is everything okay?"

She turned to find Scott standing close by. His concerned gaze brought tears to her eyes. She blinked hard to hold them back. "My mother's nurse wants me to call."

"Do you want me to call for you?"

His offer was so tempting, but she shook her head. She had to do this herself. "No. I can."

From her purse she dug out the number for the nursing home. Within a few minutes she was talking to Mrs. Angelo.

"I tried to reach your brother first. Your mother took a fall this morning."

Trista's chest tightened. "Is she okay?"

"She broke her hip. She needs surgery, but the hospital needs either yours or your brother's signature on the consent form."

With one hand, Trista rubbed at the place between her eyebrows that began to throb. "Which hospital?"

"Bon Secours Richmond Community."

"I'll be right there."

She hung up. Her mother was alive, but hurt. She had to get a message to Ross, but she didn't want to bother him now. He needed to concentrate on Kelly. She'd tell him later, after Mom was in recovery.

"What happened?" Scott asked.

"My mother fell and broke her hip. I need to go sign some papers so they can operate."

"I'll come with you."

She'd like nothing more than that. "It's not necessary."

She headed back to the waiting area. She asked Eric to let Ross know that she'd be back soon. As she headed to the elevator, Scott followed.

"I said I don't need you," she stated, wanting so badly to lean on him. But she was strong. She could do this.

"I know. I'm coming anyway," he stated.

They stepped into the elevator. "Why?"

"Because whether you want to admit it or not, you shouldn't go through this alone."

She folded her hands together to keep them from trembling. "I'm fine."

The elevator doors slid open and she marched

to her car. She tried to open the lock with her key, but her hands shook too much.

"Here," Scott said and took the key. "You're shaking so badly you shouldn't drive." He took her by the elbow and led her to the passenger door. He unlocked the door and held it open. "Get in."

"When did you get so bossy?" she asked, but was truly grateful he'd insisted .

"I've always been bossy. You just haven't seen it until now."

He went around to the driver's side, got in and started the engine.

Resigning herself to letting him take her to her mother, she slid into the seat and shut the door. After giving him directions, she settled back and stared out the side window. First Kelly, now her mother. How much more could she take today?

"Why are you really doing this?" she asked.

"Because you need a friend right now."

She glanced at him. "So today you're my friend? Not my pastor?"

"I'm both."

That was good. She could deal with that, but why did she feel vaguely empty? She told herself she didn't want more from him, couldn't ask for more from him. But still…she sighed. *Leave well enough alone, girl.*

"Has Kevin contacted you again?"

Trista snorted. "No. And he probably won't. He'll fixate on something else soon, I'm sure."

"You're very cynical."

"When it comes to Kevin, I am." Thinking about the years of emotional hurt she'd endured while married to him made her shudder.

At the hospital, Trista asked at the front desk for her mother. The male nurse directed her to the second floor. Once there, Trista and Scott were introduced to a doctor named Corbin Sterns.

"Nice to meet you, Pastor Crosby." To Trista the doctor said, "Miss Van Zandt, I'm glad you came. Your mom's stable and we've set the fracture, but your mother needs a pin to hold the bone together. It's unlikely she'll be able to walk much from here on.

"She's been in some pain, so we've given her a sedative. If you'll look over these forms and sign them, we can get her into surgery."

Trista took the forms, read them and signed where appropriate. She handed them back to the doctor. "Can I see her?"

Dr. Stern nodded. "Of course."

Aware of Scott at her heels, Trista braced herself before entering the sterile room. Her mother lay on a gurney with IVs and monitors hooked up to her arm and an oxygen tube in her nose. She moaned slightly and Trista's insides clenched with empathy.

Cautiously, she approached the bed. Her mother looked even more fragile and vulnerable than she had the previous week. Trista's chest ached as she took her mother's hand, careful not to dislodge the IV stuck into the purple vein.

"Mom. Mom, it's Trista," she said softly.

For a moment Trista thought her mother was too medicated to hear her, but then her mother's eyelids fluttered slightly.

"I'm here, Mom. Ross had to stay with Kelly. She got into an accident but she and the baby are fine. They have a little boy." Trista's voice broke. She didn't even know what they'd named her nephew.

Mom opened her eyes, her unfocused gaze on the ceiling. Trista didn't know what to do. She felt so inept. She glanced at Scott, who stood near the window. He gave her an encouraging smile and nod.

Turning back to her mother, Trista said, "Mom, can you hear me? Do you know what happened to you? You fell. They need to repair your hip. But you'll be okay. I'm here and I won't leave you."

Mom turned her head, her gaze shifting to Trista. For a moment her gaze remained unfocused, then she narrowed her eyes as if trying to focus. "Trista?"

Relief and pleasure at being recognized clogged Trista's throat. She swallowed before answering. "Yes, Mom. I'm here."

Mom nodded. "You're all grown-up. When did that happen?"

While you weren't paying attention. Bitter hurt squeezed Trista's chest, but she forced herself not to respond with words she'd only regret. "Do you know what happened?"

Mom frowned. "I fell. You just told me that."

Maybe crankiness was a good sign. "Yes. I did." Trista brushed away a strand of stray hair that had fallen across her mother's forehead. "You'll be going in for surgery soon."

Her mom closed her eyes. "I just want to sleep."

"I know, Mom. And you can. I'll be right here."

"I love you, Trista."

The air left her lungs in a rush. Tears gathered at the backs of her lids and spilled out. Her throat constricted. "I love you, too."

Two orderlies and a nurse bustled in. Trista was forced to step away and watch as they wheeled her mother from the room. Scott's hand at her elbow startled her. She turned to stare at him with awe. "She said she loves me. I can barely remember the last time she said that. If fact, I'm pretty sure I only wished she'd said those words."

"Of course she loves you, you're her daughter."

She moved away from him. "You don't understand."

"Try me," he said, his voice soft, compassionate.

He'd said he wanted to help. He claimed to be her friend and her pastor. She could use both at the moment. She refused to contemplate what else she needed from him. "My mother was a drunk. My father, too. Ross was more of a parent to me than either of them." Trista's gaze shifted to the door her mother had just been wheeled through. "I always wondered what I did that made her not love me. That made her not want to be my mom."

She glanced at Scott and the pained expression on his face made her quickly add, "I know, I know. I'm not to blame for the actions of my parents. But I'm a product of their actions. Just as my mother is a product of the actions of her parents. Last time I went to the nursing home I saw a photo album that I'd never seen before. One of the pictures was very disturbing. I think my mother had been abused by her father."

Scott briefly closed his eyes. "I'm so sorry."

She stared out the window. "Me, too."

Awareness slipped down her spine as Scott came to stand beside her. "It may be a while before your mother is out of surgery. Why don't we go the cafeteria and I'll buy you a cup of hot chocolate."

She smiled up at him, thankful for his presence. "I'd like that."

A few hours later, Dr. Stern found them sitting in the cafeteria near the window that overlooked the city. "Your mother is doing well. She's sleeping comfortably, but she will be out for at least twelve hours. I would suggest you come back tomorrow to see her."

Relieved, Trista thanked the doctor and then she and Scott headed back to the children's hospital to check on Kelly. After a brief visit with her and a quick peek at her new nephew, Trista longed to see her own little baby. She said goodbye to Scott and then drove herself to the Chestnut Grove Child Care center.

She hurried inside and stomped off the snow from her shoes. She could hear lively music coming from the main play area. At the check-in gate, Cybil Ahearn greeted her. The older woman smiled, her gray eyes warm behind her thick glasses. "Aidan's doing so well. And it was a nice surprise to meet your young man. We hadn't met before."

Trista's heart slammed against her chest wall, catapulting her breath out of her lungs. "What?"

She pushed open the gate and rushed into the main playroom. Her gaze swept over the children and landed on her son. He sat on the floor playing with a train.

Next to him sat Kevin.

Trista locked gazes with Kevin and the hard gleam in his eyes sent rivulets of apprehension cascading over her skin. The moment Aidan spotted her, he let out a squeal and crawled toward her. She scooped him up and held him close to nuzzle his neck. Her heart pounded so hard she could barely breathe.

Kevin rose and came to stand before her. He looked out of place in his dress clothes and slicked-back hair.

"What are you doing here?" she asked, keeping her voice low, but she couldn't hide her agitation.

"I came to see my son," he declared clearly without regard to the day care workers who openly stared at them.

What game was he playing? "You should have called and arranged a visit," she fumed.

"To see my own son?" He gave her a mocking smile. "I do appreciate that you had me down as the father in the paperwork. That was helpful."

Trista clenched her jaw tight. At the time she'd filled out the papers for Aidan to attend the day care, it hadn't seemed right not to acknowledge Kevin as Aidan's father. Now she wished she'd made a note stating he didn't have visiting rights.

Taking Aidan to the front entryway, she signed him out, then gathered his diaper bag and coat.

"We need to talk," Kevin stated as he followed her.

She sat on the bench and put Aidan's coat on. She glanced up at her ex-husband, noting the light of challenge in his eyes. Her stomach knotted tight. "Not here."

He nodded and grabbed a long trench coat from the wall rack before going outside. Trista breathed a sigh of relief which would be short-lived. She could see Kevin standing on the walkway.

Emily Hage, the director of the center, came out of her office. She was tall, athletic and in her mid-thirties. "Trista, is everything okay?"

"No," Trista replied tightly. "If my ex-husband comes here again, please call me before allowing him access to Aidan."

Emily's eyes widened. "I'm so sorry. Of course, we will. I had no idea. He showed his ID and he is listed on the paperwork."

Trista reined in her anger. "I know. I should

have been clear in the beginning. I didn't think we'd ever be in this situation. But we are now."

"Please forgive us. It won't happen again," Emily assured her.

"We'll see you tomorrow," Trista said gently to let her know she wasn't angry at her.

Carrying Aidan on her hip and his diaper bag slung over her other shoulder, she went outside. Kevin smiled as she came to stand beside him.

"Can I take my favorite girl out to eat?"

After the day she'd had, spending time with Kevin was last on her list of possibilities. She shook her head. "Listen, Kevin. It's been a really hard day."

"All the more reason for me to take you out," he coaxed. "We still need to talk."

"I—"

"Or I could just come to your apartment."

She had a feeling if she didn't just get this over with, she'd end up with him stalking her until she listened to his baloney. She let out a resigned sigh. "We can go to the Starlight Diner. They're kid-friendly," she conceded. "You can follow us."

She went to her little sedan and noted that Kevin climbed in a new sports car. After securing Aidan in his seat, she drove to the Starlight.

She parked and went in. Kevin joined them a

moment later. The Starlight was a retro café in the fifties style, complete with a soda fountain and lots of nostalgic memorabilia filling the walls. Trista slid into a corner, bright blue vinyl upholstered booth beneath a poster of James Dean. A vintage tune from the old jukebox played in the background.

Kevin slid in to the booth opposite her. By the expression on his face she could tell he found the place not to his taste. He picked up the menu, stared at it a moment with a pinched looked, and then put it down. "Isn't there a real restaurant in this town?"

Nothing that appealed to her had ever been good enough for him. "This is a kid-friendly place," Trista murmured as she secured Aidan in the high chair beside her.

The waitress came over. Trista ordered mac and cheese, French fries and milk with a straw. Kevin shook his head and the waitress left.

Nerves stretched taut, Trista played with her napkin. "So, Kevin, what more is there to say?"

"Plenty. I want you back."

Her gut tightened. Unbelievable. "We've gone over this." She rubbed at her forehead. "I don't trust you."

"I can earn your trust," he assured her.

Anger stirred hot and heavy. She'd tried that avenue before and he hadn't lived up to his promises. Maybe the more direct approach would get through to him. "Kevin, let me put it baldly. I don't love you anymore and I don't want to reconcile. I want you out of my life."

His jaw tightened and his eyes narrowed. "Aidan is my son."

She swallowed past the constriction of apprehension clogging her throat. "You gave up custody."

He gave her a sly smile. "I've changed my mind."

Her hackles shot to the roof and her patience with him rapidly dissolved. She said tightly, "I am more than willing to give you visitation rights. I offered that in the beginning and you refused."

"How can you do this to me?" he stammered, his complexion mottled with anger. "You came from nothing and still I married you and gave you a son. How dare you not want me back!"

Aware that his raised voice had attracted stares, she hissed, "Shh. Stop yelling." She stared at him, flabbergasted he'd be so obtuse. "You're the one who left, remember? You didn't want me or our son. You stated in a court of law that you'd been unfaithful. And now you're mad at me?"

Visibly reining in his anger, Kevin gave her a tight smile. "You'll regret this."

He slid out of the booth, then took an envelope from the inside pocket of his coat and laid it on the table. "I'll see you in court."

Trista blinked as Kevin walked away. Court? She picked up the envelope, broke the seal and stared with horror at the document, her blood freezing in her veins.

Unbelievable. She dropped the papers on the table.

He was going to try to take custody of Aidan away from her.

Scott sat at his kitchen table with his laptop in front of him. He entered the chat room at the Kingdom Room Web site, hoping to distract himself from his thoughts of Trista. She'd gone through so much today. First Kelly's accident and then her mother's fall.

He was thankful he'd been able to be there for her as her friend and pastor. But when she'd allowed him to hold her, offering comfort and support, he hadn't been acting as anything other than a man needing to protect and cherish a woman.

Not a smart thing. He simply hadn't been able to help himself.

Scrolling through the many posts to check up

on the topic of the day, he forced himself not to think about Trista. Instead, he entered into the discussion of holiday traditions and pretended she wasn't on his mind.

Chapter Ten

In the middle of the night, unable to sleep, Trista logged on to the Kingdom Room chat room and found the discussion on holiday traditions fascinating. Since her family had never had much in the way of traditions, she was gathering lots of fun and interesting ideas to do with Aidan, who thankfully was now asleep in his crib.

She'd had the hardest time putting him down tonight. He'd been overstimulated with Kevin's visit and then dinner out. And, she had to confess, she'd snuggled with him longer than normal.

Just the mere thought of losing her baby sent panicked shivers through her system. Kevin wasn't getting his way so he was throwing his version of a tantrum. One that could hurt Aidan. Her insides rolled and she fought off the nausea. She wanted to knock some sense into him, but then he'd probably have her arrested for assault.

She couldn't do anything tonight, but in the morning she'd call her lawyer and discuss the document Kevin had handed her. Though it took a lot of self-control to keep from calling Scott and crying on his shoulders. She'd done that enough for one day. She had no business getting emotionally attached to him.

A post from *Called2serve* popped up.

For the past few years I've helped serve food to the homeless. Then I go to my parents where everything is decorated to the hilt and there's enough food to feed an army. Granted with three siblings and their families, we are a small army☺ One of the traditions my grandfather started and I always insist we continue is called the Thanksgiving beans. We have a miniature pot filled with gold and silver spray-painted kidney beans. The beans are spilled out in the middle of the table, then everyone grabs a bean. Then the little pot is passed around. Each person must say what they are thankful for and then drop their bean into the pot. We do this until all the beans fill the pot.

Trista liked that idea and wrote it down on a piece of paper along with several other traditions she'd already noted, hating that she didn't have anything worthwhile to share.

Hi, all. I'm so grateful for all the wonderful traditions and holiday stories being shared here. I'm taking notes so that my child and I can start traditions of our own.

    Momof1

Momof1

    I have a friend who has some great traditions in her family. I'll ask her if I can share them with you. Have you joined any women's groups where you live? I know several mothers with young children in the town I live in have joined a group called MOPS—Mothers of preschoolers. I bet you'd find lots of ideas through a group like that.

    Called2serve

Called2serve

    Thanks for the suggestion. I'll check into it. I noticed that the stores in my area are already decorating for Christmas with evergreen boughs and lights. It's all very festive.

    Momof1

* * *

Momof1

It is festive. I love all the holiday shows that start playing after Thanksgiving. My favorite is the Peanuts Christmas. What is yours?

Called2serve

Called2serve

My favorite is *It's a Wonderful Life* with Jimmy Stewart and *Miracle on 34th Street* with Maureen O'Hara. There's nothing like the classics.

Momof1

Momof1

It's a Wonderful Life is one of my faves, too. I especially like the scene where George and Mary are dancing the Charleston and the floor opens up beneath them. I laughed so hard when they fell in.

Called2serve

Called2serve

That was funny, mainly because you could see it coming and couldn't do anything to stop it.

Momof1

From the other room Aidan let out a cry. Trista quickly posted she needed to go and then turned off the computer before heading into Aidan's room. He had pulled himself up and was standing at the railing.

"Hey, big guy, it's sleep time," she cooed as she picked him up and then sat in the rocker. Some people would say she should let him work out going to sleep on his own, but having a childhood where her own cries were never answered made Trista loath to let her son cry himself to sleep.

She never wanted him to doubt that she'd be there when he needed her. God willing. And Kevin didn't succeed in taking him away from her. Her pulse pounded in her ears at the mere idea of not being with Aidan.

As she gently rocked him, she tried to calm herself with thoughts about all the things she was thankful for; Aidan, Ross, Kelly and baby Cameron. She was thankful for her mother, something she'd never have thought possible.

And she was thankful for Scott. For his friendship, his willingness to be there for her and his steady wisdom as a pastor.

She could only pray that one day God would bring someone like Scott into her life for keeps. Because maybe with God in her life a happily-ever-after wasn't impossible.

* * *

Trista arrived at the library for Scott's meeting with Lynda a little before noon. The cold dreary day matched her mood. She'd had a long talk with her lawyer. Per her lawyer's advice, on her way to the library she'd purchased a journal to note all conversations with and actions taken by Kevin.

Her next step was to contact his parents and see if they would like to see Aidan. She didn't want to be accused of deliberately keeping the Hughes's grandchild from them.

Though the law was clear that Kevin would have to prove her an unfit mother before custody could be granted to him, this whole ordeal would prove to be an emotional roller coaster; Aidan's well-being was at stake.

Scott's sensible two-door car pulled into the parking lot. He got out and came toward her, his blond all-American good looks very appealing. She could picture him on some tropical beach with a surfboard in hand. But today he was dressed for the cold with a heavy wool coat, dark trousers and serviceable yet stylish footwear.

As he approached, his smile lifted some of her gloom.

"Hi, there," she said.

"How are you today?"

She didn't want to dump any more of her problems on him, so she shrugged. "Okay. I just hope Lynda shows."

"Why don't we wait inside for her?"

With a nod, she preceded him inside. She hadn't realized how cold she was until the warm air bit her skin and caused a tingling in her toes, fingers and nose. Scott helped her out of her parka and hung it on a rack. He followed her to the children's department where she'd met Lynda before. They sat across from each other.

"So how do you want to proceed?" Scott asked, his eyes searching her face.

"I can tell her what legal options are available, but I think she needs to hear that God isn't going to punish her. Which seems to be her greatest fear."

"Unfortunately, the church as a whole hasn't done enough to bring the domestic abuse issue to light. It's a problem too often ignored or minimized, and silence promotes the problem. I hope it's okay that I discussed the issue with Reverend Fraser. I didn't break confidentially by using names, but I needed his input."

"Hey, all the insight you can bring to the table is welcome," Trista assured him, grateful for his forethought and preparation.

"Here she is," he murmured.

Trista followed his gaze. Lynda walked hesitantly toward them. She had a scarf covering her head and her coat buttoned high. Her gaze darted to them and then skittered away as she veered off down an aisle. Trista started to rise to go after her, but Scott's hand on her arm kept her in place.

A few moments later, Lynda approached and sat next to Trista.

"I'm glad to see you," Trista said softly.

Lynda gave her a shy smile then turned her troubled gaze to Scott. "Do you know?"

There was kindness in his expression. "Yes. Trista has shared your story with me. I hope you know that I do not sit in judgment of you or your husband. I'm only here to help you and answer any questions that I can. I hope that I can alleviate any fears of God you might have."

Trista took Lynda's hand. "We only want to make you and Logan safe."

"Thank you," Lynda said. "I do appreciate your concern. I just don't know what to do." She looked beseechingly at Scott. "I made a vow before God. For better or for worse. How can I break that?"

"First, you have to understand that we are all made in God's image and possess equal worth to Him. You are no less loved or valued than anyone else. Do you believe that?"

"I guess," Lynda replied.

Trista nodded encouragingly, thinking how much she needed to hear Scott's words, as well. She'd spent so many years feeling unloved and abandoned by God, but now she was hopeful that what Scott was saying was true for her, too.

Scott leaned forward, his gaze intent on Lynda. "God never intended for marriage to give abuse license. Abuse is wrong in all its many forms. God's word tells us that violence and oppression are not His ways. He hates those who take advantage of others and will deal harshly with them on judgment day."

"But what do I do until then?" Lynda questioned, her voice barely above a whisper.

"You do what you need to do to keep you and Logan safe."

Lynda's eyes widened. "So you think I should leave him."

Scott's lips pressed together for a moment. "I can't tell you that. Only you can make that decision."

Trista gritted her teeth, wishing he'd take a stand. The woman's husband was abusing her, how could Scott not recommend she leave?

"But I want to make clear that God doesn't condone your husband's behavior. Far from it,"

Scott continued. "Colossians 3:19 clearly states that husbands are to love their wives and not deal harshly with them."

"But Ephesians also says that wives are to submit to their husbands," Lynda countered.

Scott shook his head slightly. "That is one of the most misunderstood concepts in the Bible. When the whole chapter is read and taken in its entirety as God's plan, we see how we are to live our lives in all aspects of relationship. And starting with verse twenty-one, the passage describes mutual submission within the family. Wife to husband, husband to wife. Both to the Lord, first and foremost."

"This is all very confusing," Lynda whispered.

"Scott, I think one of Lynda's fears is that she'll be breaking her marriage vows if she does anything that results in her leaving." To Lynda she said, "Is that correct?"

Lynda's gaze fell to the tabletop as she nodded.

"Lynda," Scott said gently, "God loves you. You are His precious child. He has never given anyone permission to abuse you. The abuse is the sin."

A tear slipped down Lynda's cheek and fell on the table. Trista ached for her. She squeezed her hand. "Let us help you make a plan."

Releasing Lynda's hand, Trista dug out the

journal she'd bought and tore out several pages. "First, if an argument starts make sure you move to a room with easy access to an exit." Trista wrote down the words as she said them. "Then, go to a neighbor's house and call the police."

Lynda made a strangled noise.

"Or call me," Trista amended. "We'll have a code. Say… Can we go shopping? I can come to wherever you are. And you need to have an emergency kit ready."

"Kit?"

"If you decide to leave, you'll want a change of clothes, money and documents, like social security card, insurance, extra medications for both you and Logan. Also, make sure you know right where your car keys are at all times."

Trista met Lynda's wide-eyed stare. "Have you talked with Logan about any of this?"

"No, I couldn't," she uttered. "He doesn't know."

Trista doubted that. Logan was smart; he probably knew very well what was going on. "You at least need to tell him how to call 911 if you're incapacitated."

Lynda's hand covered her mouth. "It won't come to that."

Trista held on to her patience. "It could. And you need to equip your son."

Lynda shrank a little. "Douglas wouldn't…"

"Promise me you'll do this." Trista folded Lynda's hands over the sheets of paper.

"I don't know." Lynda abruptly stood and tucked the papers in her coat pocket. "I need to leave now."

Trista's shoulders slumped as she watched Lynda walk to a shelf of books, grab a few and hurry to the checkout counter. Scott reached out and took Trista's hand, his touch warm and comforting. "She'll never leave him," she stated.

"That's not our call to make," he countered softly.

"Why not? Why couldn't you tell her to leave him?"

"Trista, she has to come to decide that for herself. If she leaves because we've told her to, then she can fall back on that as an excuse to go back. She has to be in control of her decision."

"It's just so frustrating." Anger burned in her gut. "I have half a mind to call in a complaint myself."

"That would only put her and Logan in more danger."

She sighed, hating how helpless she felt. "I know that. It has to be her decision. But when will enough be enough?"

"At this point we can offer our support and our prayers."

She slipped her hand away from his. "True." She rose. "I have to get back to work."

They left the library together. Scott walked her to her car. "How are Kelly and Cameron?"

She smiled. "Kelly will be released tomorrow. But I don't think she or Ross will leave the hospital much until Cameron can come home."

"That's understandable." Scott hesitated, hating to pry, but as her friend and as a pastor he felt compelled to ask, "Have you worked things out with Kevin?"

Trista's eyes darkened. "Not by a long shot."

"Would you like to try mediation again?"

She gave a derisive laugh. "Oh, we're going to be mediating. Only it will be in court."

"What?!"

Trista opened her car door, her eyes troubled and the line of her jaw rigid. "Long story. It's too cold out here to get into it now."

Seeing how upset she was tightened a knot of compassion in his chest. "Why don't we go grab a cup of coffee and talk?"

She shook her head. "I have to get back to work. I have a case I'm behind on, but thanks."

"Maybe this weekend?"

"I'll think about it." She climbed in. Before shutting the door she said, "Thanks for your help today with Lynda."

"You're welcome." Confused and concerned for her, he said, "I'd like to be able to help you."

"You're sweet. And you may be called upon to give a character reference for me. As my pastor and my friend," she said before closing the door and driving away.

Scott stared after her, hating the dejected and helpless feeling invading his soul. He wished she'd have confided in him. She was trying so hard to be strong and he was afraid for her, afraid she'd eventually break.

And against his better judgment, he wanted to be there for her.

Chapter Eleven

"So how do you like living here?" Rita, a mom Trista had met at the MOPs program, handed her eight-month-old son a pair of plastic toy keys from the bookstore floor after wiping them on her sweater. "It can't be easy trying to start your life over again."

"No, but it's worth it." Especially once Kevin's lawsuit was resolved. Next week was the hearing date. What a great Thanksgiving present, having to go to court to fight for her child. "I made the right move."

"Well, I'm glad you're here. And so is Jacob." Rita smiled softly. "It's always nice to make new friends."

Trista agreed. Since she'd moved to Chestnut Grove, she'd made many new friends. Scott included.

Sunday morning, however, he wasn't waiting for her at the church door, much to her disappointment, which was ridiculous. She couldn't expect him to wait for her every week.

She hustled Aidan into the nursery. An older woman with kind eyes greeted him with open arms. "There's our big guy!"

Trista's heart squeezed tight to see how loved he was and how comfortable he was with the ladies there.

In the sanctuary, she spied the Matthewses in the same spot they'd been in the last week and wondered if that was normal for people to sit in the same spot week after week. The place she'd sat was occupied so she had to sit farther back beside the Nobles. They formally introduced themselves as Beatrice and Charles Noble.

The couple were an odd match. Beatrice was tall and willowy with warm hazel eyes and short spiky hair, and flowing clothing. The balding Charles wore a plaid sport coat and looked as though he belonged more on a golf course than in church.

Again the sermon was very interesting and Trista found herself welling up with tears during several of the praise songs. The hope of God's love that had budded in her soul began to blossom and she could feel His care.

After the service she picked up Aidan and then asked the way to the youth center. She told herself she really shouldn't go search out Scott, but she didn't want to leave without at least saying hello. And that was the only reason she wound her way to the youth center.

She found Scott and several teens loading wrapped toys in big bags and storing them in a trailer behind the building.

Staying inside where it was warm, she watched for several minutes before Scott noticed her. Her heart did a little hiccup when he smiled and broke away from the teens.

"Hi. It's good to see you," he said before touching Aidan's cheek. "And it's good to see you, little guy."

"I just wanted to say hi," she said, offering up the lame excuse to see him. Her cheeks flushed with heat. "What are you all doing?"

"We've been having a toy drive all month for needy children. We're packing the toys away for safekeeping until it's closer to Christmas when we'll deliver them."

"That's wonderful." She really admired Scott's giving and caring nature. Along with a lot of other things about him that she found endearing, like his honesty and wisdom. She also liked how much he cared for Aidan. He made her think they were special to him.

Naomi Fraser came in to the youth center with a lively bounce to her steps. The woman's blue eyes sparkled when she saw them, and Trista smiled, wishing she had half as much energy as Naomi.

"Trista, it's so nice to see you again," Naomi said with a pleased smile.

"And you," Trista replied.

"I just heard the best news," she said to Scott. "Karla White is responding to her cancer treatment and may be able to come to Chestnut Grove for Christmas. And her husband, Mike, will be home on leave, as well."

"That is good news," Scott agreed. To Trista he explained, "Karla is Alex Donovan's cousin. He has had custody of her two kids while she's been at a cancer treatment center in Philadelphia and Mike's been in Iraq. Naomi's oldest daughter, Dinah, is engaged to Alex."

Empathy grabbed at Trista. Her own problems seemed petty and not worth worrying about in the face of what this family had to deal with. "Praise God."

Naomi beamed. "This Christmas will be spectacular. With my son living in town and Dinah engaged to Alex. Even Ruth, my youngest, will be home from her freshman year of college."

Trista envied this woman's children. She envied the pride in Naomi's voice and the excitement in her eyes. A ribbon of sadness unfurled inside of Trista. It was too late for any of that with her own mother. But thankfully, not too late for her and Aidan

Still Trista held her mother's declaration of love like an early Christmas present.

"Has Scott invited you to help with the Thanksgiving dinner here at the church?"

She nodded, remembering she had put off giving him a commitment when they'd first met. "Refresh my memory, please."

Scott inclined his head. "We host a dinner for the poverty stricken and the homeless here on Thanksgiving day. We serve a hot meal, provide a blanket and scripture packets. So many people in the community come out to help. We get started around eleven in the morning and end around three so that people can go home to be with their families for the rest of the day." His eager expression called to her. "We sure could use more help."

It sounded wonderful, but also a bit overwhelming. How could she help and watch her son? "I have Aidan. I don't—"

"Oh, honey. Bring him," Naomi interjected as she made goo-goo eyes at Aidan. "We have lots of little ones around and plenty of teenagers to help watch them."

She swallowed. "Teens?"

Naomi gave her a knowing glance. "All Red Cross certified babysitters. I promise."

Since Kelly and Ross would most likely be at the hospital, and since she couldn't take Aidan there, Trista saw no reason why she couldn't help at the church. "I think I'd like that."

"Great. We'll see you on Thursday," Naomi said before bustling away to supervise the kids.

"She's a whirlwind," Trista commented.

"She is. But she's great. Her family is the best," Scott replied.

Trista heard wistfulness in his voice. She wanted to soothe that hurt she sensed in him. She remembered what he'd said about being the black sheep of his family because he'd gone into ministry rather than a professional career like the rest of his siblings. She ached to think he didn't feel loved or accepted by his family. "Do you see your family on Thanksgiving?"

"Yes. I go there after we're done here. I'd never live it down if I didn't go."

"Well, it's good they wait for you."

He shrugged. "They don't need to. I don't enjoy it."

His unappreciative attitude irritated her. "Take it from someone who didn't have much of a home life growing up—you should cherish every moment you get with your family no matter how trying."

He raised his brow. "So the tables are turned now, huh? You're giving me advice?"

"That's what friends are for," she quipped.

"True. Thank you. I needed to hear that."

Her irritation dissolved. "You're welcome."

"Have you told Ross about your mother?"

"Yes. He checked on her and she's doing as well as can be expected. I plan to take Aidan for a visit on Thanksgiving morning."

"I'm sure she'd appreciate that. I'm proud of you for making the effort."

Warmed by his praise, she admitted, "I've spent so many years resenting and hating her, that I'm not really sure what to feel about her now."

"Forgiveness would be a start," he said gently. "She was wounded and acted out of that wound."

It hurt to imagine what horrors her mother may have endured. "I know. I've been praying about that. Praying that she finds peace. That I find peace."

"That's great."

The look of approval and joy in his eyes, sent her pulse fluttering. She thought he was great.

He studied her face. "Tell me what's happening with Kevin?"

Ugh! Talk about a mood killer. "I don't need to burden you with that," she replied.

Every time she thought about the possibility of losing Aidan, her heart clutched and her breathing tightened.

"Let me help. That is what friends are for," he coaxed.

It would be a relief to let some of her anxiety out. And Scott could help her process through her emotions and thoughts. "You're right." She looked around. "Where could we talk privately?"

"How about we go to the nursery room. You can set Aidan up with some toys."

"Perfect."

Scott led her to the now-deserted nursery. He spread a blanket on the floor while she pulled out some toys from the bins. Sitting cross-legged on the floor next to Aidan she watched Scott stretch out his long legs and lean back on his hands.

"What did you mean the other day when you said you were going to court?" he asked.

A flash of anger followed closely by fear shot

through her. "Kevin served me papers. He's going to try to sue for full custody."

"You're kidding! I thought he gave up custody in the divorce?"

She gestured her bewilderment with one hand. "He did."

"That's insane," Scott said, his voice laced with anger.

Trista pushed a toy train with her finger, making the little engine move toward Aidan. His chubby fingers reached out and grasped the toy. "Kevin doesn't really want Aidan. He's doing this out of spite."

"How can you be sure?"

"I know him." Her mouth twisted with resentment. "He claims to want our marriage back, but not once has he apologized, not once has he said he loves me or Aidan. He wants control back."

"Good thing you're an attorney."

She gave a wry smile. "I'm in litigation. Besides, I'm not arrogant enough to represent myself. I've retained the best family law attorney in the state of Virginia."

"That was smart. What do you think the court will do?"

"The judge will do what's in the best interest of the child." She stroked Aidan's head, her nerves somewhat soothed by the downy softness of his dark hair. "They'll look at the fact that Kevin left his family and has had little contact since. They'll interview family and friends. There will be home visits by court-employed social workers and a Guardian Ad Litem, which is a court-appointed attorney that will advocate for the child."

Her voice hitched with dread. "If they think that it's in the best interest of the child to take Aidan from both of us, they will until this is settled."

"The court could take Aidan?"

His horrified expression matched the horror the thought produced inside of her. "Worst-case scenario, but yes."

She rolled her tense shoulders. "I'm glad Aidan isn't old enough to understand what's going on. But someday he will be. And if Kevin doesn't win custody now, he could come back and try again at any time. This is a threat that will hang over Aidan and me until Aidan turns eighteen."

Scott shook his head, his eyes wide. "I had no idea. What about joint custody?"

She scoffed. "I told you. This isn't about Kevin wanting to be with Aidan. I've offered visitation rights. He refused. This whole thing is about him wanting to hurt me." As if he hadn't already taken his pound of flesh before. But thankfully, now she was stronger and no longer emotionally vulnerable to Kevin.

"I will be praying about this," Scott stated with determination.

Grateful for his support and knowing that his prayers lifted up with her own would be more effective, she said, "I'd appreciate that."

His eyes lit up. "I'm so glad to hear that. Prayer is a powerful thing. God loves for His people to pray."

She was one of His people. The thought brought a sense of welcomed peace. "You said I should try church and...I have. I'm finding myself very drawn to God and what I've been learning."

A young teenage boy stepped into the room. "Pastor Scott?"

"Hey, Jeremy. What's up?"

"We're done loading the trailer."

"I'll be right there."

The boy ducked out and Scott rose. "I better go."

Trista picked up the toys. Sad that their time was at an end, yet grateful for the relief of sharing. "Thanks for listening."

"My pleasure. That's what I'm here for," he said and reached for a toy just as she did.

Their hands met, and the contact sent pulsing sensations up her arm. She lifted her gaze to his. His blue eyes stared at her intently. She could lose herself in his clear and inviting gaze.

Okay, not good. He was her friend, her pastor.

But at the moment she wanted him to be more. She wanted a man to lean on and be open with in all aspects of her life. She wanted her dream of happily-ever-after. Unfortunately, Scott was off-limits.

He'd already established that fact when he'd qualified their relationship as friend and pastor.

She released her hold and stepped back. "I'll finish up here."

He swallowed, the strong cords in his neck visibly working. "Okay. Let me know if I…uh, can be of more help."

"I will, thanks."

"See you Thursday," he said and bolted from the room.

Picking up Aidan, she muttered aloud, "Why am I always attracted to guys that don't want me?"

The Tuesday of Thanksgiving week, Ross ignored the murmured voices of the nurses in the neonatal unit of the Children's Hospital as he stared at his son in the sterile incubator, hating the tubes running out of Cameron's small body. Useless rage choked the breath from his lungs. Ross curled and flexed his fingers. He was going to nail the person who did this to a high pole.

Despite Zach's pressure to back off the investigation Ross had continued his search for Wendy Kates and who had paid Harcourt so much money to keep quiet about the baby girl.

The Bon Secours Richmond Community Hospital where Wendy had given birth had microfiched their records but because they dated more that forty years ago they hadn't inputted them into a computer yet. Ross had asked Eric to go to the records department and search for Wendy's medical records. Eric had discovered that Wendy Kates had died in childbirth. Her body had been cremated and buried in Richmond.

Another seemingly dead end.

Except one notation by the doctor, indicating there had been blunt trauma to the head, nagged at Ross. How had she sustained an injury to the head while giving birth? Had the injury occurred during delivery? Was someone trying to cover up Wendy's death? Or had she gone into labor because of the blow to the head? Who had hit her? The unnamed father of the baby? And where was that baby now?

Questions, questions and more questions.

"Ross?"

He turned to see Trista standing just inside the neonatal unit. She was dressed in a very professional-looking two-piece dress suit with black pumps and her dark hair was pulled back into a fancy twist. Her coat was draped over her arm. Her eyes looked grim and there were lines bracketing her mouth.

He went to her and gave her a hug. "Put on a gown and come in."

"I can't right now. I have to be in court in a few minutes, but I need to talk with you first."

They stepped out into the hall. The overhead lights cast a green glow over her complexion. "Are you okay?"

She made a face. "I wasn't going to burden you with this, but I figured you should hear it from me before you hear it from someone else. Kevin's suing me for custody of Aidan."

Feeling as though he'd just sustained an electrical shock, Ross shook his head. "What did you say?"

"I know. It's ludicrous, but I'm on my way to the preliminary hearing now."

He stared at her. "When did this come about? You haven't said anything about Kevin for months."

She grimaced. "I didn't want to worry you, and then Kelly had her accident and mom broke her hip—it's just been too much for you."

Ross ran a hand through his hair. "Kelly and Sandra went for coffee. They should be back any moment. I'll come with you as soon as they return."

"No," she protested and placed a restraining hand on his arm. "I can handle this. You take care of your family."

"But you are my family."

"And believe me, I'm thankful you're my big brother. But today I need to stand up for myself."

Ross clenched his fists. "I'll strangle him when I see him."

One side of her mouth lifted in sardonic amusement. "I share the sentiment, but I don't think that would be a good idea." Her gaze grew earnest and beseeching. "But you could say a prayer that all goes well."

"I will." He hugged her again, wishing he could take care of this for her. "You call me if you want me there, okay?"

"You bet," she assured him then glanced at her watch. "I better run. I'll come back to see Cameron this afternoon."

He watched his little sister walk away. He was

so proud of who she'd become. For a few years she'd been so rebellious and out of control that he'd doubted she'd make it, but somewhere along the way she turned into a woman of substance.

A few moments later, Kelly, Sandra and Pastor Scott pushed through the stairwell door.

Seeing Ross in the hall, Kelly rushed forward, her arm with the broken wrist in a sling across her body. "Is Cameron okay?"

"Yes, he's fine. Trista was just here. Kevin is suing her for custody."

Kelly's eyes widened. "Oh, no. Can he win?" Kelly asked.

Ross shook his head. "Doubtful. He'd have to prove her an unfit mother. Which won't happen. But still I should be there with her at the hearing."

"Of course you should," Sandra agreed. "I'll stay here with Kelly and Cameron."

"She doesn't want me there," Ross stated and realized that not being needed by Trista hurt a little.

"Well, someone should be there with her," Kelly said, her gaze shifting to Scott. "Did you know about this?"

"I did," he said. "Trista confided in me on Sunday. And as her pastor I couldn't break that confidence."

Ross saw the gleam in Kelly's eyes as she tilted her head and stared at Scott. "Is that all you are to her? Her pastor?"

A flush crept up Scott's neck. "That's all we can be."

"Why?" Kelly asked and planted her good hand on her hip.

"It's complicated?" he said, almost as if he were seeking the answer himself.

Ross had a feeling there was more going on between his sister and the young pastor. And he approved. "I sure wish Trista wasn't going through this alone."

"She won't be alone. I'm going over there," Scott stated firmly.

"Go now, then," Ross directed.

Scott nodded and headed for the elevator, his loafers making soft squishy sounds as he went.

Kelly hooked her arm through Ross's. "Are you trying to do a little matchmaking?"

Ross gave her a lopsided grin. "I'm just looking out for the welfare of my family. And it couldn't hurt to have a pastor on her side in the eyes of the judge."

"Right," Kelly agreed. "Let's pray the judge sees the truth."

Chapter Twelve

With its gleaming hardwood floors and arched doorways, The Chestnut Grove courthouse gave Trista an odd sense of the past. The building had been built in the late 1800s and though there had been modern updates in the plumbing and electricity, the detailed craftsmanship had maintained its beauty.

But today, Trista's nerves were strung too tight to appreciate the architecture.

"Sit down, Trista. Pacing isn't helping."

Trista paused and turned her attention to her lawyer, Nora Daley. Trim, professional and sharp-eyed, Nora exuded controlled confidence. Her blond bob framed her oval face and bright green eyes to perfection. Her smart-looking tweed pantsuit was stylish yet understated. Trista wished she could be as calm, but Nora's life wasn't on the line. If Trista lost Aidan, she didn't think she could handle it. *Please, Lord, let this end well.*

"I'm too keyed up to sit," Trista said as she resumed her pacing. In ten minutes they would go before the judge. Trista shivered with dread and apprehension. No matter how much Nora reassured her, she still felt vulnerable.

It was just like Kevin to use his family's money and influence to push the hearing up so soon. What if the judge decided Kevin would be a better provider for Aidan? Her stomach rolled with dread.

To stay sane and to avoid heaving what little she'd managed to eat that morning all over the floor, she shoved that thought away. She was armed with her journal and she would make sure the judge knew Kevin's true motives for his actions today.

"Trista."

She spun around to find Scott walking toward her, looking good in his tan suit and geometric patterned tie. Her heart did a double take and pleasure at seeing him leaped through her. "What are you doing here?"

"Your brother asked if I'd come and offer my support," he replied.

"Oh." Disappointment dampened her joy. He

was here simply out of duty. Her pastor, her friend. Nothing more. "That was sweet of him and sweet of you for coming."

"He's worried about you," he said.

She searched his gaze, hoping to see his feelings about her, but his direct gaze was sincere and polite. She acknowledged his words about Ross with a nod. "Scott, this is my lawyer, Nora Daley. Nora, Pastor Scott Crosby."

Nora rose and extended her hand. "Nice to meet you, Pastor. It certainly won't hurt to have you here."

"Good. I want to help in any way I can," Scott replied.

The door to the courtroom opened and the uniformed officer motioned for them to enter.

Trista's stomach rebelled and for a panicked moment she was sure she was going to throw up. Scott's comforting touch at the small of her back calmed and settled her as he guided her into the room. She followed Nora to one of the tables at the front facing the judge's bench. Scott sat on the bench behind her.

Another man came in a moment later and moved to the other table. Trista recognized the man as Kevin's lawyer, Ted Argus. In his midfifties and balding, Ted resembled one of Trista's high school teachers.

Trista glanced at the door wondering why Kevin hadn't arrived yet. Typical. The man had no regard for anyone else's time. Not even a judge's.

When Judge Harvey Komorow entered the room a few minutes later and took his seat behind the huge wooden bench, Kevin still hadn't shown.

"Hughes vs Van Zandt in the custody of Aidan Hughes," the judge intoned as he read from the document in front of him. He looked up, his lined face falling into a frown. "Is the petitioner and the respondent here?"

Nora stood and replied, "The respondent is, Your Honor."

Ted slowly rose, his gaze darting to the door. "Uh, Your Honor, I'd like to request a continuance."

Judge Komorow raised his bushy black-and-silver eyebrows. "Am I to take it the petitioner is a no-show?"

Ted tried not to grimace, but his uncertainty was clear. "I'm sure he'll be here soon, Your Honor. This is very important to my client."

The judge huffed. "Well, if it were important then I would assume your client would be here." Judge Komorow turned his attention to Trista. "Are you the mother?"

On shaky legs, Trista rose. "Yes, Your Honor."

"And the child in question lives with you currently?"

"That is correct, Your Honor."

The judge shifted his attention back to Ted. "Mr. Argus. I suggest the next time you choose to take up this court's time, you will make sure your client is present. Is there anyone here who would like to speak on behalf of either party?"

"I would, Your Honor," Scott said as he stood.

Trista's heart melted to her ankles.

"And you are?" the judge asked.

"Pastor Scott Crosby of Chestnut Grove Community Church," Scott replied, his voice clear and strong.

"Well, Pastor Crosby, speak."

"I would like the court to know that Trista Van Zandt is a loving and devoted mother. Aidan is well cared for. Trista is a caring and generous woman. This court should not even contemplate taking Aidan from his mother."

Trista's eyes misted at the unexpectedness of Scott's words.

Judge Komorow inclined his head. "Duly noted. Now, Mr. Argus. Since your client still has not shown and I see nothing in these documents to support a change of custody, it is the ruling of this court that the petition for sole custody filed by

Kevin Hughes be dismissed." The judge banged his gavel and departed.

Swamped with relief, Trista sagged back into the chair as soon as the judge disappeared. The ordeal was over. Thankfully, Kevin had shown his true colors.

"Well, that was easy," Nora stated as she picked up her briefcase.

"Thank you," Trista said, tears burning at the back of her eyelids.

"Honey, don't thank me. Your ex shot himself in the foot. The court has a long memory and will use his actions today against him in the future if he tries this again," Nora replied. Scott moved to stand beside Trista. Nora inclined her head. "Pastor, it was nice to meet you."

"Likewise," Scott replied.

Nora waved goodbye and left the courtroom. Scott held out his hand to Trista. "Let's celebrate."

Trista took Scott's hand and allowed him to pull her to her feet. With regret, she said, "I can't. I have to get back to work."

"Right."

"Thank you for today. I've never had someone other than Ross ever stand up for me." She squeezed his hand with affection. "I can't begin to tell you how much that means to me."

"I care about you and Aidan," he stated, his gaze direct.

The little girl inside of her jumped with joy. He said he cared! She swallowed back the yearning to have him take her in his arms. Just because he cared didn't mean anything more than that. "I…we care about you. You're a good pastor and a dear friend."

One side of his mouth tilted up and he released her hand. "Right. Glad to be of service."

As they left the building, Trista had the uneasy feeling that she'd somehow offended Scott.

She wished how he felt didn't matter to her so much.

Thanksgiving Day arrived in a flurry of activity for Scott as the church prepared to feed the homeless. First he helped the youth set up rented banquet tables and chairs in the youth center.

Townspeople arrived to help serve the food, and a line of the homeless and poverty-stricken formed outside the building. The freezing temperatures made Scott take action. He had Jonas Fraser and Alex Donovan usher the people into the sanctuary where it was warmer to wait.

As the morning turned into afternoon, Scott's thoughts returned to Trista again and again. His pulse always picked up speed when he thought of her. He hoped her visit with her mother was going well. She'd been nervous about taking Aidan there when he'd talked with her last night.

Although he'd used the excuse of the church dinner to call her, he'd really just wanted to hear her voice. He enjoyed the soothing tones and the way talking to her came so easily.

And when it came time to say goodbye, he hadn't wanted to hang up. He was becoming attached to her. And to Aidan.

That was a problem.

She only thought of him as her pastor and friend. He'd set that boundary himself for both their sakes, but the more he got to know her, the more he wanted to be with her. Now he wanted to erase the boundary and start over.

He wanted her to see him not only as a pastor and friend, but as a man.

"Hey, Scott." Eric Pellegrino called from the doorway of the youth center. "We need some help in the kitchen."

Scott hefted his end of a table into place. "Be right there."

He left the teens to finish up and followed Eric into the kitchen where covered dishes donated by the church members filled all the available counter space. Scott recognized Mrs. Lumly's flowered

Crock-Pot and he hoped the green dish was Mrs. Avery's sweet potato pie.

Scott had learned after the first year not to sample too many of the dishes because he'd end up feeling like a stuffed turkey.

Eric's girlfriend, Samantha smiled her super-model smile. Tall, gray-eyed, the former model had returned home to small-town life not that long ago. "As you can see, we have an abundance of food and thought maybe we should start putting some out on the tables. But we weren't sure if you had a specific order or plan in mind."

"Whatever you two think will work best is fine. I'll send the kids in to help," Scott replied, his stomach rumbling from all the delicious smells wafting up from the dishes.

He left Eric and Samantha to their work and then sent several teens in to help.

"How about we put the buffet tables along the back wall," said Reverend Fraser.

"That'd be great," Scott replied. "Jeremy and Andy, can you help?" Scott called to two of the older teens. Between the four of them, they made short work of placing the tables.

Naomi gathered a patchwork selection of loaned tablecloths to put on the buffet tables. She set to work as soon as the tables were set.

"Hello, hello." Sandra Lange breezed in rolling a cart full of pies in front of her. "I hope fifty pumpkin pies will be enough."

"Plenty," Naomi said and directed Sandra to the last buffet table. "We'll have them start at the other end and finish here with your pies."

Scott went to the kitchen and gave the go-ahead for food to be brought out.

Soon the buffet table was laden with savory foods and behind each dish stood a church member ready and waiting to begin serving. Excitement bubbled in the air. Scott motioned for Alex to escort in the masses. Hungry men, women and children of all ages formed a line at the front of the buffet table.

Reverend Fraser and Scott walked around visiting with the people as they took their plates to the table to eat, offering encouragement and prayer. A reporter and photographer from the local newspaper were in attendance, as well, snapping pictures as the reporter interviewed several people.

Scott kept an eye on the door, expecting to see Trista arrive. Finally he noticed her standing just inside the doorway, holding Aidan. His heart tightened with gladness. Her gaze searched the crowd and landed on him. Her face broke out in a smile and she waved. He hurried to her side.

"Hi. I'm so glad you came," he said.

She gave him a tentative smile. "Me, too." Aidan pumped his chubby legs and wiggled in her arms. "I should get him to the nursery."

"Let's go. Several of the high school girls are watching the little ones. They're all very responsible kids," he assured her as he led the way to the nursery where one of the teens, Nikki, took Aidan and cooed over him.

"This okay?" Scott asked Trista, waiting to see if she'd be okay with the arrangement.

After a moment, she nodded. "He loves all the attention and everyone seems to love him."

Scott sure did. He'd fallen for the little tyke the first time he'd seen him.

Satisfied that Trista was okay leaving Aidan in the high schooler's care, he led her back toward the youth center. "So tell me how your visit with your mother went."

Trista's smile lit up the hallway as she stopped. "Really well. Mom fawned over Aidan. I thought at first she might have been confused, thinking that Aidan was Ross as a baby, but then she told me I did good and that she knew I'd be a good mother."

The tears misting Trista's eyes brought tenderness welling up in Scott. "And you are."

"Your confidence means a lot," she stated.

He wanted to tell her she meant a lot to him but he kept silent. If he spoke, he was sure to tell her how much she'd come to mean to him. Until she gave him a sign that she wanted more from him than spiritual guidance and friendship, he wouldn't put himself or her in an awkward position.

"We also stopped at Kevin's parents' house."

Scott gaped. "Really?"

"I'd thought a lot about what you said about building bridges and I didn't want to be accused of withholding their grandson from them."

"And how did that go?"

"Surprisingly well. They were smitten with Aidan and totally want to spoil him."

"Will they try to take Aidan from you?"

She shook her head. "No. I think being grandparents is going to suit them just fine."

He was relieved for her and Aidan's sake. "Well, that's one of the great things about grandparents. Naomi is always saying she can't wait to spoil some grandbabies."

"As long as I can be there to temper the effects," she stated.

"Smart woman."

"You know, the Hugheses were a lot different today than in the past. When Kevin and I married, they'd made it clear they didn't think I was good enough for their son. But apparently, Kevin stopped by to see them the other day with a woman in tow. I guess I'm pretty good in comparison."

He stared. "What?"

"I know." She made a "you got me" face. "While we were waiting in the courtroom for him, he and this woman were sailing off to the Bahamas. I explained to his parents what had been going on and they were very upset. They even apologized for him and invited Aidan and I to have Christmas dinner with them at the country club."

Relieved that Kevin was truly out of the picture for now and that Trista had some closure with the Hughes, he stated, "It's been some day for you."

She nodded. "They want to take Aidan and I Christmas tree shopping next weekend."

He grinned. "See, didn't I tell you building a bridge would be worthwhile?"

"I'm very grateful for your wisdom," she replied as she touched his arm.

Warmth seeped into his veins and he wanted to take her fully in his arms. But a simple touch was not enough of an indicator that she would welcome his attention. "Uh, we should get back."

Her gaze met his. "Yes, we should."

But she didn't move. Neither did he. Scott stared into her blue eyes, seeing affection and caring that left him breathless. What he saw had nothing to do with him being her pastor or friend....

A commotion from inside the youth center shattered the moment. They hurried to see what was going on.

A camera crew had invaded the youth center. Douglas Matthews, dressed in a slick navy pin-striped suit and a red paisley tie, stood with a microphone in his hand as he interviewed Reverend Fraser.

Nothing like a town celebrity to liven up things.

"Ugh! That man," Trista whispered. "I wonder where Lynda is?"

Scott captured her hand and gave her a squeeze. "We've done what we can. What Lynda decides to do is in God's hands."

"I'm not giving up on her," Trista stated with a note of defiance in her voice.

Scott appreciated how much she cared and wanted to stand up for someone who obviously wasn't standing up for herself. "And I'll help as much as I can."

She squeezed his hand back. "We should probably get to work, too, don't you think?"

"Definitely."

Scott led Trista to the buffet table. Sandra Lange smiled her welcome and handed Trista a pie cutter. Giving Trista a parting smile, Scott visited with the men, women and children sitting at the many tables.

Something clattered to the floor.

"Oh, you oaf!" Douglas shouted to a bedraggled man who stood staring at the plate of food now splattered all over Douglas's shoes. "These are Italian. Do you have any idea how much they cost? You've ruined them!"

The photographer snapped off several shots of Douglas's outraged face.

"Hey, you better not print those," Douglas screeched.

Scott tightened his jaw as he and Naomi rushed to help defuse the situation. But Douglas stormed out with his camera crew in tow. Naomi helped the man who'd dropped his plate get another. And Scott cleaned up the mess on the floor.

"Here."

Scott looked up to see Trista kneeling beside him with a wad of paper towels. Pleased by her help, he said, "Thanks."

He could get used to working with her by his side.

Together they wiped up the spilled food.

"That man is some piece of work," Trista said as she tossed the soiled towels in the trash.

"He has a temper that he doesn't seem to be able to control," Scott agreed.

"I'm worried about Lynda. You don't think he'd take his anger for this incident out on her, do you?"

"I pray not, but maybe you should use the office phone and give her a heads-up."

"Good idea." Trista hurried away.

Scott went back to visiting but quickly broke away when Trista returned a few minutes later.

"She was thankful and promised to stick to her safety plan if he came home in a rage." Trista sighed. "I hope she really will. I offered to come over there now, but she adamantly refused."

"We'll check on her a little later," Scott promised.

They went back to the previous tasks and Scott found his gaze continually seeking her out as she served pie. Her popularity with the people didn't rest solely on the pie she handed out, but on the kindness she showed as she chatted easily with those in line. Several times she met his gaze and offered him a smile which made him feel as if he could fly.

The afternoon wore down and the youth center cleared out.

"Hey, what are you and Aidan doing after we're

done here?" Scott asked as Trista wiped down a table.

She shrugged. "Going home, I guess."

"Would you be interested in joining me at my parents'?" He held his breath, hoping she'd say yes.

She blinked. "I…I'm not sure that's a good idea."

"Why?"

"It's just…" She cocked her head to one side. "Well, why do you want me to?"

He couldn't exactly tell her that he was falling for her so he settled for another truth. "I could really use a buffer with my family."

Empathy darkened her blue eyes. "You came with me to see my mother so I should repay you the favor."

Disappointment slid through his chest. "I'll take that. Would you like to ride over with me or do you want to follow in your car?"

"We can move Aidan's car seat into your car, if that's okay?"

"Of course." He watched her move away to finish clearing the tables. He admired her loyalty and giving nature and really enjoyed her honesty and forthrightness. He only hoped that one day the barriers between them could be breached.

Scott took out the trash and then went to his office to call his parents.

"Scott, when are you coming? I've been holding dinner," groused his mother.

Scott sighed. "Soon, Mom. And if you don't mind, I'd like to bring two guests."

"Oh." There was a moment of silence. "Someone I know?"

"Not yet. We'll be there within the hour."

"Fine. I'll set two more places."

"Uh, Mom. One of them is a baby."

"A…baby?" she said into the phone and then her voice became a bit muffled as she spoke, "Scott's bringing home a person with a baby."

Scott could hear voices in the background and he winced, but better to get the ribbing over with now than in front of Trista.

Something clicked. His sister came on the line. "Scott! Is there something you're not telling us?"

"No!" He rolled his eyes at the outrageous suggestion. "It's just a friend." At least for the moment.

"Are you bringing the mother or the father?"

"Yes, dear, do tell," his mother added, sounding intrigued.

Great, now he had both of them on the line. "The mother. Her name is Trista. We'll be there soon. Please treat her nicely."

His mother huffed. "As if we'd do otherwise!"

"Really, Scott. Of course we'll welcome her. She does know you're a pastor right?"

Scott closed his eyes. "Yes, she does."

"Well, then that's a relief. We wouldn't want another Sylvia catastrophe."

Rubbing his hand over his face, Scott replied, "No, we wouldn't. Trista is well aware of who I am."

"And she still likes you?" his sister trilled. "That's wonderful."

Gritting his teeth, he said, "Yes. Well. I've got to go."

"Your father wants you to stop and pick up more eggnog. You know how he likes his eggnog," his mother said before hanging up.

Scott put the receiver back in its cradle, already exhausted from his family, and he hadn't even been ribbed yet by his brothers or grilled by his father. He could only pray that Trista would understand that the Crosby clan could be overbearing and overwhelming. But they were still his family.

Hopefully, they wouldn't scare her off before he had a chance to tell her how he felt.

Chapter Thirteen

Scott pulled up in front of a huge white house with green trim and a white picket fence. Trista straightened, both intrigued and intimidated. This was a house straight from her childhood dreams.

Dreams that had never come true.

She glanced at Scott. No wonder or awe showed on his face. But of course not. He'd grown up here, this was familiar. Nothing special. She wished she knew what that felt like.

Well, maybe today she could pretend. Not only for Scott's sake. But for her own, as well.

As Trista lifted Aidan from his car seat, the front door opened. A woman in her midsixties stepped out and wiped her hands on the red apron at her waist. Her long, faded blond hair was held back at the nape of her neck by a gold clip and her snowman-print sweater was very festive. For a moment Trista thought she'd stepped into an episode of *Leave It to Beaver*.

Mrs. Crosby moved down the porch stairs to greet them. "You must be Trista," she said, her smile warm and inviting and her eyes crinkled at the corners.

"Yes. And this is Aidan," Trista replied.

"Oh, he's adorable. Scott, you didn't tell me how adorable the baby was." Shifting her gaze to Trista, she asked, "May I hold him?"

Awed by Mrs. Crosby, Trista nodded and handed Aidan to her. Aidan touched the woman's face eliciting a giggle from her. "Oh, you precious darling. I must show you off."

Mrs. Crosby went inside, leaving Scott and Trista by the car.

Scott shook his head. "We'll have to pry him from her hands I think. My mother loves children. Come on. Let's get this over with."

His words surprised her. How could he dread coming home? She'd give anything for this welcoming, caring environment. It was so extremely different from what she'd grown up with.

But unfortunately dreams and reality rarely mixed.

Just look at Lynda Matthews.

Trista would bet she'd never expected to find

herself abused and intimidated by her husband. Worry gnawed at the back of Trista's mind. When Scott had stopped to pick up the eggnog, she'd taken the opportunity to call the Matthews home. The housekeeper had informed Trista that Mrs. Matthews was not at home. Trista wished she knew that Lynda and Logan were safe.

But as Scott had pointed out, Lynda was in God's capable hands.

Trista followed Scott into the house and glanced around with awe. Everything was just as she imagined, warm and cozy with knickknacks and comfortable-looking furniture.

"Ha! Checkmate!" one of two men sitting at the chessboard near the fireplace exclaimed, drawing Trista's attention.

"You cheated!" the other man stated loudly.

"No more than you."

"I'm done."

"Poor loser."

An older man whom Trista decided must be Scott's father rose from the recliner.

"Hello there, young lady," he said and held out his hand. "Joseph Crosby." His big strong hand engulfed hers.

"I'm Trista Van Zandt. Thank you for allowing my son and I to come for dinner."

Mr. Crosby's lined face broke into a smile. "Always glad to have company. This one never brings home a guest. Ashamed of us heathens I think."

"Dad!" A red flush crept into Scott's cheeks.

Trista stiffened, ready to be offended for Scott but then she noticed the twinkle of teasing in Mr. Crosby's pale-green eyes.

The two chess players came to stand beside Mr. Crosby. Trista stared at the two handsome men, seeing the family resemblance in their thick blond hair and green eyes. But these two looked almost identical.

"Twins?" she asked.

The brothers exchanged an amused glance. "We get that a lot," the brother on the right said. He held out his hand and shook Trista's hand vigorously. "John. I'm fourteen months older than this lug and five years older than that squirt."

"I'm Kyle." The younger of the two took her hand and brought it to his lips for a soft kiss. "The charming one."

Easing her hand back, Trista glanced at Scott. His jaw was set tight and the glare he was giving his brother could ignite a fire.

"You're also married," Scott stated flatly.

Kyle winked at Trista. "Doesn't mean I'm dead."

A little taken aback by his unabashed flirting, Trista raised an eyebrow. "What does your wife think of that?"

"Oh, I'm quite used to his outrageous self," a petite redhead said as she descended the staircase, her intelligent hazel eyes gleaming. She came to stand beside her husband, who immediately tucked her against his side and swiftly kissed her before grinning at her like a smitten child.

The redhead smiled at Trista. "I'm Lydia. We're so glad you came."

"Thanks," Trista replied, instantly liking Kyle's wife.

Mrs. Crosby came in carrying Aidan. "Okay, everyone, Ana and I are ready to get this show on the road. We've waited long enough for Scott to arrive. It's time to eat."

An olive-skinned brunette came out of the kitchen, her hands laden with dishes. John rushed to her side, took her burden from her and placed them on the table. Then they disappeared back into the kitchen.

"That's John's wife, Ana," Scott said as he escorted Trista toward the table. "They've been married for almost twenty years."

Impressed, Trista nodded as she reached for

Aidan. Mrs. Crosby gave him a squeeze before releasing him.

"Joe, honey, will you go to the garage and grab the high chair," Mrs. Crosby said as she moved back toward the kitchen.

Mr. Crosby saluted her retreating back then grinned at Trista. "I have my orders," he said before walking away.

"Where's Elise?" Scott asked. To Trista he said, "My sister."

Kyle held out a chair for Lydia. "She and Ryan are downstairs with the kids. I better go round 'em up." Kyle came around the table and put Scott in a headlock. "You better come with me. Elise is gonna want to grill you like steak on the barby, especially when she gets a load of the beauty you brought home."

Trista bit her lip to keep from laughing. She could see the embarrassment in Scott's eyes at his brother's teasing. Scott managed to get out of his brother's hold, then gave Trista an apologetic smile before following his brother out of the room.

"Don't mind them," Lydia said as she leaned forward. "They love to tease each other, and especially poor Scott. He doesn't take it so well."

"I noticed," Trista replied. "Why is that?"

Lydia shrugged. "Being the youngest, he was

always the brunt of their mayhem. I grew up just down the street so I got to see it all."

"So you and Kyle are childhood sweethearts?"

That elicited a laugh. "No. We hated each other growing up. He was the class clown and I was the—" she waved a hand at her bright red hair "—the joke."

Trista frowned as she sat in the chair Scott had pulled out for her before he'd left the room. Settling Aidan on her lap, she pushed the silverware away from his clapping hands. "They made fun of you?"

"Oh, they make fun of everyone. It's a family trait. All except Scott." Lydia picked up her water goblet and took a drink. "Kyle and I didn't get together until college. We had a debate class together." Her eyes sparkled. "That was fun. We used to tease each other unmercifully, until the teacher finally made us work together on the same team. We credit Professor Sorenson with starting our romance."

"Wow, that's a cool story," Trista smiled, imagining what that must have been like to watch.

A noise like a herd of elephants on rampage filled the air. Suddenly the dining room was swamped with chattering and laughing bodies. Children ranging from elementary school age to teens scrambled for spots around the large dining table, leaving random empty chairs for the adults. Lydia introduced Trista and the kids rattled off their names so fast there was no way Trista would ever remember any of them.

A boy of about seven sat on Trista's right, Garen, Trista thought he'd said. And a teenage girl sat on her left where Trista had expected Scott to sit. Mr. Crosby came in with the high chair and had the boy scoot his chair over so he could place Aidan next to her. They all laughed at Aidan's antics as she secured him in his seat.

A blond woman whom Trista assumed was Elise, stopped beside Trista and put a hand on her shoulder. "Hi, I'm Elise." She grinned, looking giddy. "I'm so glad you're here."

Overwhelmed by this big welcoming family, Trista's mouth grew dry and she blinked back sudden tears. This is what she'd wanted for herself. It was what she wanted for her son.

"Now look what you've gone and done, Elise," a tall raven-haired man with a thick mustache said as he tucked a napkin into the collar of a boy who looked like a small replica of himself. "You made her cry. Scott's going to think twice about bringing home girls."

"I'm not—" Trista stuttered and blinked rapidly.

She caught the embarrassed look on Scott's face as he took a seat across the table from her. She swallowed to regain her voice. "I'm very glad to be here, as well. You all are so welcoming, it's a bit overwhelming."

Mrs. Crosby came in just then. "Here now, are you all torturing our guest?"

"Auntie Elise made the lady cry," explained the girl with dark red pigtails from the other end of the table.

Mrs. Crosby tsked. "Leave her be. Joe, come get the turkey." The two disappeared back into the kitchen.

The teenage girl sitting beside Trista leaned close. Her big green eyes and wide smile showed her lineage. "I'm Beth. Don't mind them. They'll settle down soon. I always warn my friends when they come over to be prepared and not to take anything anyone says personally." She sighed as her gaze strayed to Scott. She lowered her voice. "Uncle Scott's not so keen on it."

Very perceptive girl, Trista thought as she watched Scott talking with a preteen boy on his right.

Beth added, "Neither is Johnny." She pointed her finger to a boy who sat in the end seat. His dark head bent forward, his gaze downcast.

Trista's heart went out to the boy. He seemed so out of place among the boisterous clan. "Is he okay?"

Beth giggled. "He's reading. Look under the table."

Making a show of dropping her napkin, Trista bent and gazed down the length of legs to Johnny's. Sure enough an open book lay in his lap. She straightened. "That's one way of escaping the chaos," she murmured.

John and Ana came back out of the kitchen with more dishes. Mrs. Crosby carried in a carving knife while Mr. Crosby placed a huge golden turkey on the table. Taking the carving knife from his wife, he laid it on the table, as well. Then he took his wife's hand. She in turn, took the person's hand next to her, and so it went around the table. Trista met Scott's warm gaze. She wished he was sitting beside her so she could hold his hand.

"Scott, why don't you say the blessing, since that is your job," Mr. Crosby said, his voice crisp.

Scott blinked, breaking eye contact before bowing his head. He spoke in a gentle and reverent tone.

After the blessing, the meal was a whirlwind of bowls and plates being passed and laughter and conversation blending into its own special music.

Aidan dug his fingers into the mashed potatoes and smeared them all over his face, much to the younger children's delight. Trista ate so much she thought she'd pop.

As the feast wore down and the plates and the soiled table covers were cleared away, to Trista's amazement, everyone resumed their seats. She'd expected the children to run off to play and the adults to return to the living room. Elise gave Trista a clean rag to wipe up Aidan and Ana provided some toys for him to play with.

Mrs. Crosby brought out a medium-sized plant pot decorated in harvest colors. Something clinked inside the pot before she dumped the contents on the middle of the table. Pebble-sized pieces of silver and gold slid down the polished wood table.

A flurry of hands reached for them. Beth placed several in front of Trista before pushing a large handful farther down.

Trista picked up one and examined it. It looked to be a painted lima bean. Her heart sped up as she lifted her gaze to Scott. He pensively fingered a bean.

"Trista, this is a family tradition that started with my grandparents and has continued on," explained Mr. Crosby. "Everyone takes some beans and then we pass the pot around. As we drop a bean inside, we say what we're thankful for." He dropped a bean in the pot. "I'm thankful for my family." He passed the pot to John who sat on his right.

Realization hit Trista in a flash. Her gaze jumped to Scott as ribbons of excitement unwound through her. He glanced up and cocked his head in question at her. She was too far away to speak to him, but she was going to bust if she couldn't say something soon. The pot landed in front of Scott. He dropped in his bean and said, "I'm thankful...for Trista."

There were giggles around the table. Trista could feel her cheeks heating and pleasure filled her heart. Finally, the pot came to her. She picked up a bean and placed it inside. "I'm thankful to be here."

She passed the pot on. It went around several more times. By the last pass, the sentiments had become hilarious. Johnny dropped his bean in and announced, "I'm thankful for Captain Underpants books!"

Trista laughed so hard her sides hurt. Eventually, the kids left and most of the adults drifted away to turn on a football game in the living room or help in the kitchen.

Trista rose, thinking to offer her help in the kitchen, as well.

Scott sat in the chair vacated by Beth. "Don't go."

Trista sat back down and grinned. "I joined MOPs."

"Excellent! Elise and Lydia both belong to the local one here," he said.

"Well, a friend advised me to."

"Smart friend." His bright blue eyes glowed with interest, but not an inkling of connection.

"A friend I met online," she singsonged.

That got his attention. "Online?"

"And this friend told me about this great family tradition of the pot with the beans."

She grinned with delight as realization lit his eyes. She wondered what he'd say if she told him she was falling in love with him. The knowledge of that thought took her breath away.

"You're *Momof1*?"

"Yes," she said a little breathlessly. "And you're *Called2serve*."

He laughed. "That's too funny. Wait until I tell Naomi."

"Tell Naomi what?" Kyle pulled up a chair.

Trista and Scott exchanged glances. "Nothing. Private joke," Scott said.

"Oooh. You have private jokes? That's how it starts," Kyle said with a cunning grin.

"Go away," groused Scott.

Lydia came up and sat on her husband's knee. "Is he bothering you two?"

"Yes," said Scott.

"No," said Trista at the same time.

Lydia laughed. "Well, I need to borrow him a moment." To Kyle she said, "The kids want to play air hockey but can't get the thing to work."

Kyle stood, picking up his wife in the process. "Okay, you two. Don't do anything I wouldn't do."

Lydia giggled as he carried her away.

"I'm sorry about that," Scott said, his expression exasperated.

"No need to apologize." Trista took his hand. "You have a great family who loves you very much."

"Yeah," he scoffed.

She squeezed his hand. "I see it even if you can't. All their teasing and little gibes are not out of disrespect."

"It sure feels like it," he said, his gaze downcast.

"I think that's because you take it that way. Trust me. They all love you."

Scott wanted to believe her. "Well, I'm still a disappointment."

"How can you say such a thing?"

"You heard my dad," he said. "Because it is your job," he intoned in a deep voice, mimicking his father.

"Well, it *is* your job. And he didn't say it with any type of disrespect or disapproval in his tone." She stared him in the eye, direct and stern. "You're being too sensitive."

Leave it Trista not to pull any punches. Was he being too sensitive? He'd never been comfortable with rough play or practical jokes. He'd always found his brothers' sense of humor slightly offensive and could never understand how Elise put up with them.

"Son?"

Scott looked at his father who stood near the staircase. "Yes, Dad?"

"Can I talk with you for a moment?"

A stab of worry pierced his gut. "Uh, sure." Scott said to Trista, "I'll be right back."

Scott followed his father upstairs to his study. The room hadn't changed much since Scott was a child. Degrees and diplomas hung on the walls as well as family photos taken over the years. His dad's desk was covered in medical journals and papers. His dad sat at his desk, pushed some papers aside and then fired up his desktop computer.

"Have a seat," Dad said.

Unsure what was going on, Scott sank back into the leather recliner in the corner. The scent of his father's aftershave clung to the worn leather bringing back memories of days when Scott had hid in the study to avoid his brothers. He'd loved to curl up in the recliner and read.

Now he braced himself as Dad swung around to look at him.

"I want to talk about the anniversary party," Dad explained. "The others are planning stuff, all that frou-frou kind of thing your mother loves. I was thinking we could renew our vows and you could officiate."

Scott's mouth opened. "You want me to?"

Dad cocked his eyebrow. "Well, who else would I ask? You're the pastor in the family."

Stunned pleasure left him speechless for a moment. He found his voice. "I'd be honored, Dad."

"Good." Dad sighed. "Could you look at this and tell me what you think? I wrote this for your mother for our anniversary."

This unexpected turn of events made Scott's knees wobble as he got up and came over to the computer to view an open document. As Scott read the words his father had written tears burned the back of his eyes. His father had written a letter that told how much he loved his wife and his children, naming each child and telling a bit about what he loved about them. A tear slipped unchecked down Scott's cheek as he read what his father had said about him.

> My son Scott, who brightens the world with his compassion and empathy, has been a source of joy for his mother and I. We thought we were done having children when Scott came along. But he brought this family closer together and continues to be a source of light in our lives.

"Is it too mushy?" Dad asked, his voice holding a note of uncertainty.

Choked up, Scott could only shake his head.

"Okay, then." Dad closed out the program.

Scott cleared his throat. "Dad, why did you want me to look at it?"

His dad scoffed. "You think one of those bozos downstairs would give me an honest answer? As it is, they'll be ribbing me until I'm in the grave for writing something so mushy. I'd rather wait until after I read this to your mother before I take the hits."

So Dad didn't fully enjoy the teasing, either.

"Mom's going to love it," Scott said, feeling closer to his dad than he'd ever felt and needing to ask, "I hope that this means I'm no longer a disappointment to you."

His father's eyebrows rose clear to his hairline. "Excuse me? Disappointment? Where'd you get a lamebrain idea like that?"

Stunned, Scott couldn't come up with an answer right away. Was Trista right that he'd been too sensitive? "You always pushed me to be like the others."

His dad rubbed his chin. "I did push you. Not to be like your brothers but because your mother and I worried about you. You were always such a sensitive kid, getting your feelings hurt over things that the rest of us didn't understand. Your mom and I spent many sleepless nights afraid of how the world would treat you. I wanted to make sure you were strong. I never meant to make you think you were a disappointment."

Years of resentment and anger melted in Scott's veins as if his father's words were a powerful lamp of light. "I don't know what to say."

"There's nothing to say," Dad stated and rose to wrap Scott in his big, strong arms.

Scott hugged his father back fiercely. "I love you, Dad."

"I love you, son. And I'm proud of you." He

eased Scott out of his embrace and then gently socked him in the arm. "Now, that we've gotten the mushy business over with, we better get back or they'll think we're up to something," Dad said as he headed out the door.

On the landing to the stairs, Dad stopped and faced Scott. "Just so you know, I like your friend."

Scott smiled wide. "Me, too."

Dad clapped him on the back nearly knocking him down the stairs. "She's a keeper, son. Don't let this one get away."

Alone on the landing, Scott leaned against the wall. His spirit felt light and his head was spinning. His father was proud of him. He wasn't a disappointment.

And Dad approved of Trista.

Now all Scott had to do was sweep Trista off her feet.

Scott came down the stairs to see John and Aaron, his oldest teenager, wrestling on the living room floor. Trista sat on the couch with Aidan sound asleep on her shoulder.

Near the fireplace Johnny stretched out on the floor reading a book. Scott's dad bent to ruffle the boy's hair before disappearing into the kitchen. Johnny combed down his hair with an impatient hand.

Scott blinked as memories came flooding in. How many times as a child had Scott sat in that same place and had his father walk by to ruffle his hair?

Too many to count.

And Scott had been impatient and irritated, thinking his dad had only wanted to bug him, but Scott realized it was his father's way of showing his love in a simple, unmushy gesture. Scott decided he'd take Johnny for a walk later and make sure the boy understood their crazy family idiosyncrasies.

But first, there were matters of the heart to be taken care of.

Scott took the seat on the couch next to Trista. She immediately touched his hand. "I received a text message from Lynda. She and Logan are okay."

He turned his hand to capture her fingers. "That's a relief."

Her gaze dropped to their clasped hands. "Yes, it is."

Leaning closer, he asked softly, "Hey, I was wondering if you'd have dinner with me tomorrow night?"

She stared into his eyes. "Dinner?"

He nodded, holding his breath.

An excited light entered her gaze. "Like, as in a date?"

He grinned. "Yeah. Like, as in a date."

She grinned back. "I'd love that."

"Woohoo. The squirt has himself a date!" John exclaimed as he pinned his son to the floor.

Instead of getting irritated at his brother's invasion of his personal space and privacy, Scott grinned and said, "Yes, I do."

And he'd found the woman of his dreams.

* * * * *

In December, don't miss
Jillian Hart's A HOLIDAY TO REMEMBER,
the final book in A Tiny Blessings Tale.

Dear Reader,

I hope you found this latest installment of *A Tiny Blessings Tale* an enjoyable read. Trista and Scott were complex characters that had so much personal growth to go through before they could begin the journey together toward happiness.

This book had so many issues that I found difficult and fascinating all at the same time. Any time I delve into a character, I want to learn everything I can about the issues they face. Research is half the joy of writing. And if I have made mistakes, know that they are purely mine and I'm all too human.

I hope you will look for the last installment of *A Tiny Blessings Tale* next month.

And until we meet again, may God bless you always.

QUESTIONS FOR DISCUSSION

1. Out of all the books you could have chosen, why did you choose *Giving Thanks for Baby*? The cover? The back cover blurb? The author?

2. Did the book live up to your expectations? Why or why not? Did the story keep you engaged? Were the descriptions and setting vivid and realistic?

3. Were Trista and Scott believable characters? What did you like or dislike about each? Did the romance build believably?

4. Were the secondary characters interesting? How did they add to the story?

5. Did you read the previous installment in the series? Do you plan to read the next? Why or why not?

6. What did you think about Trista's faith journey? Do you agree that we tend to make our faith more complicated than it is? Have you asked Jesus into your heart?

7. What traditions does your family have for the holidays?

8. Have you ever helped feed the homeless? If so, share how that experience was for you.

9. Did the author's use of language and her writing style make this an enjoyable read? Would you read more from this author?

10. What will be your most vivid memories of this book? What lessons about life, love and faith did you learn from this story?

INTRODUCING

Love Inspired.

HISTORICAL

A NEW TWO-BOOK SERIES.

Every month, acclaimed
inspirational authors
will bring you engaging stories
rich with romance, adventure
and faith set in a variety
of vivid historical times.

History begins on **February 12**
wherever you buy books.

Steeple
Hill®

www.SteepleHill.com

TITLES AVAILABLE NEXT MONTH

Don't miss these four stories in December

A DROPPED STITCHES CHRISTMAS by Janet Tronstad
A special Steeple Hill Café novel in Love Inspired

For Carly Winston, telling her friends the truth about her home life was a huge step. But playing Mary in the local Nativity play gave her courage she never thought she'd have. And spending time with grill owner Randy Parker made her feel like a star.

A HOLIDAY TO REMEMBER by Jillian Hart
A Tiny Blessings Tale

Memories of wartime held former soldier Jonah Fraser captive. Yet single mom Debra Watson gave him a reason to smile for the first time since returning from Iraq. With a matchmaking teen on the job, this was sure to be a holiday he'd never forget.

HEART OF THE FAMILY by Margaret Daley
Fostered by Love

Why didn't big-hearted social worker Hannah Smith like him? Dr. Jacob Hartman couldn't figure it out, but Hannah's dedication to foster children touched his heart. If only he could find a way to get to hers.

THE HEALING PLACE by Leigh Bale

Dr. Emma Shields was Mark Williams's last hope to heal his little girl. And Emma was determined not to let their past history or her own heartbreaking loss stand in the way of a cure. With faith she'd find a way.

LICNM1107